He'd no more than stepped foot into the mercantile when a young man barreled through the door, shouting about a woman in labor and needing an ax.

Eric mounted up and rode along to the MacPhersons. He'd returned late last evening and hadn't met any townsfolk yet. How many of Reliable township's inhabitants were hillbillies? Would they all cling to the misguided ways and silly notions he'd seen Polly employ yesterday?

He didn't have to coax Polly into stepping aside to treat her family; he had to completely take away the business she and her mother ran. Quite literally, only God knew what they'd done to patients in the name of medicine. This was going to take finesse. Tact. Prayer. But Eric knew then and there he couldn't sit back and permit backwoods myths and folklore to be the basis for curing people in the modern age.

Times were changing. These people would, too—even if he had to nudge them. It was his duty, because he'd taken an oath. Nothing—and no one—would stop Eric Walcott from keeping that pledge. Not even some pretty little wheat-haired, wide-eyed, whiskey-dispensing girl.

CATHY MARIE HAKE is a Southern California native who loves her work as a nurse and Lamaze teacher. She and her husband have a daughter, a son, and two dogs, so life is never dull or quiet. Cathy considers herself a sentimental pack rat, collecting antiques and Hummel figurines. In spare moments, she reads, bargain hunts, and makes a huge mess with her new hobby of scrapbooking.

Books by Cathy Marie Hake

HEARTSONG PRESENTS
HP370—Twin Victories
HP481—Unexpected Delivery
HP512—Precious Burdens
HP545—Love Is Patient
HP563—Redeemed Hearts
HP583—Ramshackle Rose
HP600—Restoration
HP624—One Chance in a Million
HP648—Last Chance
HP657—Love Is Worth Finding

Don't miss out on any of our super romances. Write to us at the following address for information on our newest releases and club information.

Heartsong Presents Readers' Service
PO Box 721
Uhrichsville, OH 44683

Or visit www.heartsongpresents.com

Handful of Flowers

Cathy Marie Hake

Heartsong Presents

To nurses and doctors everywhere, whose dedication transcends long hours and lousy pay. So many of them reach out their hands in the name of the Lord and minister with loving care. God bless you one and all.

Also to Elvera Smith, my mama—a nurse who brought up both of her daughters to be nurses.

A note from the Author:
I love to hear from my readers! You may correspond with me by writing:

Cathy Marie Hake
Author Relations
PO Box 721
Uhrichsville, OH 44683

ISBN 1-59310-712-9

HANDFUL OF FLOWERS

All scripture quotations are taken from the King James Version of the Bible.

All of the characters and events in this book are fictitious. Any resemblance to actual persons, living or dead, or to actual events is purely coincidental.

Our mission is to publish and distribute inspirational products offering exceptional value and biblical encouragement to the masses.

PRINTED IN THE U.S.A.

prologue

1889, Chance Ranch, just outside San Francisco

Heart pounding, Polly Chance lay stark still as the door whispered open and shut. From her bed in the loft, she couldn't see who'd let himself in. Midnight darkness shrouded the cabin. Whoever it was, he moved silently as a coyote.

She slid her fingers under her pillow to grasp the knife she kept there. Mama Lovejoy had given her that knife the day she turned nine. She'd taught Polly how to use it for gathering plants, but Daddy took her aside and told her to keep it beneath her pillow each night for safety's sake. Her fingers curled around the bone handle.

"Polly!" a whisper sounded from down by the door.

She bolted upright in bed and hissed, "April, you near scared me out of my mind! Why are you sneaking around at this time of the night?"

Laurel grumbled from the other side of the bed, "What does time have to do with it? A lady never sneaks anywhere."

Polly lit a lantern and stared down at her cousin, who had moved to the center of the small cabin. April stood there dressed in her deep blue robe. Frills from her pale pink flannel nightgown peeped from the neck and hem, but the satchel by her bare feet captured Polly's attention.

"I'm running away." April fussed with her robe's belt until she tied it into an absurdly huge knot. "Either you let me stay with you, or I'm going to mount up and ride over to the

MacPhersons'. They'll take me in."

"Couldn't you wait 'til morning?" Laurel yawned. "Things always are better in the daylight."

"They'll be worse in the daylight!" April burst into tears. "I got up to visit the outhouse and found Cole at the table, reading my diary."

Laurel vaulted over Polly, scrambled down the ladder, and enveloped April in a hug. "You poor girl!"

"If I don't move in with Polly," April said tearfully, "I'll never have any privacy."

Polly slipped the knife back under her pillow. The unsettled rhythm of her heart no longer came from fright; it came from the knowledge that her well-ordered, comfortable existence had just slipped out the door when her cousin came in. Climbing out of bed, she realized the wisdom behind one of Daddy's sayings. *Nothing ever stays the same, but changes are always for the better if given to God.* She took hold of the lantern, handed it down to Laurel, and lifted the hem of her buttercup flannel gown. As her instep found the next rung to the ladder, she said, "Let's have some tea and talk this over."

It didn't take any time whatsoever for Polly to decide what type of tea to brew. Though she kept an appreciable array of teas from the times she went gathering with her mother, only one tea would do under these circumstances: chamomile. It soothed.

Huddled across the table, hands curled around her teacup, April asked, "Will you let me move in?"

"If she moves in," Laurel said, "so do I."

"Can't we worry about you some other day?" April sniffled. "Come morning, Cole is going to blab to everyone what I wrote!"

"Whatever did you write?" Laurel asked.

Polly wondered, too—but she tamped down her curiosity. "That's none of our business. Diaries are personal. Don't you worry about Cole. He owes me a favor. I'll take care of him."

"Cole owes you a favor?" Laurel and April said in unison.

Polly pressed her lips together and shrugged. From an early age, she'd learned the value of discretion.

"Well, that takes care of that." Laurel giggled.

"I'm still not living under the same roof with him. I can't bear it!" April took a gulp of tea, made a face, and dumped in more sugar. She stirred it with such agitation, the tea sloshed over the brim and formed a puddle in the saucer. "The older boys are in the bunkhouse. It's only fair for us girls to have a cabin."

Polly sat in silence. Laurel often spent the night with her already. If April moved in, Kate would, too. Literally overnight, Polly would be assuming responsibility for three younger, sometimes flighty girls. *Lord, You gave me fair warning this was going to happen. I figured it would be another year or so, but we'll just put it in Your hands.*

"It's Polly's cabin, really." Laurel cast a look up at the loft where she'd been sharing Polly's bed. "I mean, well—"

"Everyone calls it my cabin," Polly said slowly, "but the Chance family shares. We always have. Maybe this needs to be the girls' cabin. The only problem I see is, it seems unfair to leave Kate out."

"You're right," Laurel agreed.

April's eyes filled with tears. "This isn't fair. You know Uncle Titus won't ever let Kate live here."

Pouring more tea, Polly chose her words and modulated her tone just as Mama had taught her to. Often the lessons on healing folks applied just as well to dealing with them. "Once you move in with us, April, Kate's bound to want to be here, too."

"I can't blame her," Laurel admitted. "The odds around this

place are abysmal. We girls are outnumbered something awful."

Polly nodded. "I'll tiptoe over and have a little talk with Cole." On her part, the decision was already made—if only her aunts and uncles would agree with the plan, this would become the girls' cabin. The Chance families all lived in a large rectangle of cabins so their daughters would be close by—but the Chance men lost their famed logic when it came to protecting their daughters. *The last thing we need is to rile them from the start.* "April, did you leave a note for your folks to let them know where you are?"

"No."

Laurel let out a squeak. "Aunt Miriam will be devastated!"

Polly snorted. "Uncle Gideon's the one who's going to have a fit and fall in it. First off, we're going to put a note on the table for them. We need Uncle Gideon's help to reason with Uncle Titus, or Kate is doomed."

"We ought to pray," Laurel said.

April let out a short, teary laugh. "All I can think of is that saddle tramp who came through here last summer. Remember how he'd shake his head and say, 'God help us all'? Well, that's how I'm feeling."

"I like that. It's heartfelt, and we're praying it with respect." Polly put down her cup, reached across the table, and clasped both of her cousins' hands. She bowed her head. "Lord, we're blessed with a big family, but there are times it's hard to put up with them. Give us patience and humor. We'd like to ask You to make straight the path with the family so they can let us unite together here in this cabin. Thank You for all You do for us, and help us to be Your servants. In Jesus' name. Amen."

She looked up at her cousins. In unison, they said, "God help us all."

one

a week later

"We gotta make tracks. Eunice drops her young'uns faster each time." Uncle Mike shuffled nervously in the doorway. "Last one didn't take from dinner to supper."

Polly didn't respond. Mama Lovejoy had taught her to hold her tongue when her comments might cause anxiety.

"Do you"—Laurel's voice went shaky and high—"need me to come along and help?"

Polly cast a quick glance at her cousin. In the days since they'd joined her in the cabin, Laurel, April, and Kate had all offered to assist her on sick calls. They'd certainly taken to heart their pledge to stick together and help one another out, but Laurel blanched to the color of dandelion fluff at the mere mention of anything medical. She'd be in the way. "Thanks for the offer, but Aunt Tempy will be there to help. Maybe you could. . ." She thought hard to concoct some other task.

"She can finish sewing the blanket whilst April and I make lunch," Kate cut in.

"We'll be praying for you," April tacked on as she gave Polly a push. A second later, mounted atop Blossom, Polly clutched her brown leather healer's satchel and did some praying herself. Riding fast as the wind alongside Uncle Mike, Polly followed the prayer with a mental rehearsal of the necessary steps to follow for safe delivery.

They reached the MacPherson ranch, and one of the men

9

swiped her from her mount. "We was scart you might not make it in time." He didn't even bother to set her down. Instead, the hulking man carried her straight to the doorstep and shoved her inside.

Aunt Tempy met her with a quick hug and whispered, "Lovejoy's not coming?"

"Daddy said he'd bring her soon as she got home from seeing someone who's ailing."

Tempy grinned and nodded. "You know what to do. I've boiled water aplenty for ye. Lois'll be watching the other young'uns whilst we welcome this one."

Polly appreciated Aunt Tempy's confidence in her. A prayer she'd heard her mama say ran through her mind, and the words rang deep and true. *Lord, use my hands. You created this little life—now help me bring it safely into the world.* She set down her satchel, then rolled up her sleeves as she approached the rocking chair. "So how far apart are your pains, Aunt Eunice?"

"Middlin' far. I—ooohhh."

From the outside of the house, a deep male groan sounded.

After having been through other births here, Polly knew the MacPherson men made it a habit to stand directly under the window and "share" their wives' travail. At the moment, Aunt Eunice arched her head back against the pressed-wood oak rocker as the pain washed over her. When it ended, she mopped her brow with the edge of her shawl. "Guess I'd best change that to middlin' close. These pains got a fearsome grip on me when they come."

Polly nodded. Aunt Eunice didn't complain unless she had cause. "Did Uncle Hezzy bring in the ax yet?"

Her aunt let out a weary puff of air. "I been a-keepin' it under my bed, but that knothead took it out to chop wood, and now he cain't 'member where he left it!"

Supposedly, the ax cut the pain of childbirth—not that Polly believed it much after seeing women in their travail—but Aunt Eunice certainly put store by that tale. Thinking quickly, Polly pasted a smile on her face. "Well then, it's a good thing I just sharpened my gathering knife. You never saw such an edge on a blade. I don't aim to be boastful, but it could shave a gnat's whiskers. It'll do the trick." She pulled the knife from her sheath, held it up for show, then went over and slid it under the bed.

"I don't have me much time to ponder on whether that'll do," Aunt Eunice choked out before she started to moan again.

Polly splashed some whiskey onto the table and wiped it down. The pungent odor made her nose twitch, but she'd read all about Lister and knew the value of ridding her working surface of bacteria. From the looks of things, she had no time to scrub the table with lye soap.

As Aunt Tempy laid out a little blanket, diapers, a gown, and a tiny cap for the baby, she whispered, "Good thinkin' on that knife. You know how stubborn Eunice is when she catches 'old of a notion. She refused to get into bed until Hezzy found the ax. I was a-feared she'd birth the babe in the chair and drop him on his head!"

Polly flashed her an understanding smile, then opened her satchel. The MacPherson men and women stayed true to their culture from back in Hawk's Fall and Salt Lick Holler. Their more-mythical-and-magical-than-medical notions might have made sense thousands of miles away in the secluded mountains and hills, but here they amounted to amusement at best and danger at worst. No use trying to argue with a laboring woman, so Polly simply honored their traditions and went ahead with the more important preparations. She knew full well once she got Aunt Eunice upright, the baby would arrive, so she wanted everything ready first. . .if the baby cooperated.

A small vial of precious ergot came first. She carefully measured a few purplish-black scrapings onto a tiny china plate. After the delivery, she'd rub that on Aunt Eunice's gums and inside her cheek to keep her from bleeding too badly. Next, she took out the pale yellow towel she'd boiled and spread it on the table, then unrolled the necessary instruments.

"Reckon that knife'll have to do." Aunt Eunice twisted her shawl in one hand as she gripped the arm of the rocking chair with the other. "This babe ain't gonna wait for nuthin'."

"Have you decided on names yet?" Polly helped Eunice from the rocking chair and walked her toward the bed.

"No. I'm too old for this nonsense," Eunice panted. "Thirty-eight. My oldest ought to be carryin' on the line 'stead of me goin' through this."

"In the Bible, Sarah had baby Isaac, and she was much older than thirty-eight." Polly rubbed her aunt's back when the woman stopped for the next pain.

Aunt Eunice let out a gusty sigh after the contraction passed. "Ain't no questionin' the Almighty's plan. You ken how much I love every one o' the babes He give me."

"Yes, I do." Polly helped her into the bed.

Grabbing Polly's arm, Aunt Eunice whispered, "But I got me a dreadful feelin'. Thirteen's a rare bad number."

"I told her to go ahead and have another to make it fourteen, but she didn't appreciate that one bit," Aunt Tempy said as she fluffed the pillow.

"Mercy!" Aunt Eunice curled up and clenched harder on Polly's arm. A lifetime of kneading bread lent her bone-bruising strength. "Oh, Lord a merrrcyyy!"

"Dear God in heaven!" Uncle Hezzy prayed loudly from outside the cabin, "Holp my Eunice. Don't let her be a-hurtin' so bad."

Aunt Eunice's eyes narrowed as she chuffed air. When she finally relaxed, she hollered, "Hezekiah MacPherson, don't you go askin' the Almighty to do His side of a bargain when you shirked your own. Git yerself out there and find me that ax!"

Polly doubted Uncle Hezzy would leave the vicinity. Then again, everyone else in the entire clan would search high and low on his behalf. Judging from the exam she did, Polly figured they'd better hurry, because Aunt Eunice was right. This baby wasn't going to wait.

"I done decided onct this here babe comes, I'll—ohhh, hit's too hard on me," Aunt Eunice whimpered. She sucked in a deep breath and hollered, "I cain't do it 'less I got me that ax."

"Ever'body's lookin' for it, Lambkins!"

Rolling her head to the side, Aunt Eunice muttered, "Ain't that jest like a man—letting his woman labor and his young'uns work, and there he stands, pretendin' a few fancy words'll—ahhh, mercyyy!"

Fifteen minutes later, Polly laid a just-wiped-clean newborn into her aunt's arms. "A girl, Aunt Eunice! A pretty little redhead."

"Now praise the Lord!" Aunt Eunice smiled wearily. "Leastwise, I got me another daughter. Reckon 'twas worth it, after all."

"You would have said that about a son, too," Aunt Tempy said.

"Gotta set your mind to bein' satisfied with whate'er the dear Lord give ya," Aunt Eunice said as she put the babe to breast. "Kickin' 'gainst what is don't make it no different; jest gives you sore toes."

"She takes after you," Aunt Tempy said. "Lookie at that hair."

"I prayed for mercy. That's why she looks like me," Aunt Eunice said. "A girl-child who took after Hezzy would grow up to be a lonely old spinster."

"Uncle Hezzy is handsome on the inside—that's what counts most," Polly said as she tended to matters.

"Yore mama got herself a good man, and you got yoreself a good daddy," Aunt Eunice said in a crooning tone to the baby. A tired smile chased across her face, and she whispered, "And I hollered an extry bit so's Hezekiah will let me stick with the name I had my heart settled on 'stead of the one he wanted."

Aunt Tempy and Polly muffled their laughter.

"My girl-child's gonna be called Elvera. Did you ever hear a more beautiful name?"

"Elvera," Polly repeated. She'd been prepared for something unusual. Aunt Eunice and Uncle Hezzy argued over names and managed to have created some doozies. Elvera rated as one of the nicer ones. "We could shorten it to Elvie or Vera, too."

"Nope. Nobody's gonna cut down a perfectly fine name. Couldn't take an ax to the pain, and they ain't a-gonna take an ax to her name." Aunt Eunice bobbed her head emphatically. "My mind's made up."

"I got one! I got one!" The shout sounded over the thunder of horses' hooves. "Here. Take this in with you." A second later, the door opened, then shut, and someone cleared his throat.

Polly hastily flipped the sheet over Eunice and turned around. She frowned at the handsome stranger standing there. "Thank you for the ax, but we're about done here."

The tall, dark-haired stranger shoved the ax off to the side and rumbled, "Axes don't belong at a delivery. Someone handed it to me, but it's not needed." He peeled out of his coat, then stopped cold when the baby started to whimper. "He's here?"

"Yes, she is." Polly tried not to laugh at the man's horrified expression. "All ten fingers and toes."

"Only because you didn't have the ax," the stranger muttered. Instead of looking relieved and making a quick getaway, he rolled up the sleeves of his snowy shirt, baring muscular forearms. "Now then, let's make sure everything else is—"

"Hold it right there, mister." Aunt Tempy parked herself in front of him and glowered. "You don't belong in here."

"I'm Dr. Walcott."

"We're pleased to make your acquaintance," Polly said crisply, "but a man doesn't belong at a birthing."

Aunt Tempy folded her arms across her chest. "Everything's swimmin' along, right as a tadpole in a water hole."

"I'm gratified to hear that." He pushed past Aunt Tempy. "I'll just have a look—"

"No, you won't." Polly couldn't fathom the arrogance he displayed. "Mother and child are both in my hands, and—"

"And if someone competent doesn't see to matters, they'll just as likely be in God's hands within the week."

"I got me my niece and my sister-in-law here. I'm farin' better than after any of my other birthings."

"And we're glad they were here to help you," the doctor said smoothly. Stubborn as could be, he reached the bedside. "However, a woman who's had several children and is your advanced age—"

"You a-callin' me old?" Aunt Eunice nearly shouted, "I'm only thirty-seven! I got plenty of years left in me and pr'bly two or three more babes, too."

"Right now, I need to be concerned with Aunt Eunice and this baby." Polly pivoted to the side to block him. Under any other circumstances, she'd find it entertaining that her aunt had just shaved a year off her age, but right now, other matters were more pressing.

Aunt Eunice shot her a look of relief. "Doc, you cain step back outside 'til after my Hezzy sees his young'un. 'Tis fittin' for a man to see the child he fathered afore anyone else does."

"The father can come in and see the babe. I'll tend you," the doctor announced.

Polly looked over her shoulder at him. "Doctor, we don't know you from Adam. Now's not a good time for introductions. You need to honor Aunt Eunice's wishes."

"He's upsetting me. If my milk a-curdles, I'll know who to blame!"

The doctor frowned at the collection of instruments on the table, then looked at Aunt Tempy. "You must have some basic knowledge; else you'd not possess these things. The multiparous woman is likely to hemorrhage. Ergot—"

"Whoa. You're talking to the wrong woman." Aunt Tempy pointed at Polly.

The doctor's gray eyes widened in frank disbelief.

Polly sought to assure him she'd anticipated the need to administer ergot. "I have scrapings from rusty rye."

"Hit come from Hattie back home in Salt Lick Holler," Aunt Eunice said. "None better. Now you scat."

The doctor's jaw clamped shut. He nodded curtly, turned, and left.

two

Eric Walcott left the cabin and practically got mobbed.

"What're you doin' out here?"

"Git back in there and holp my Eunice!"

"Is sommat a-wrong?"

Plenty's wrong. That woman in there could be bleeding to death, and all she has is a few well-meaning, backward family members who don't understand the danger and are too steeped in ignorant folklore to accept help. Only Eric couldn't face these worried men and children and tell them those harsh truths. To add to the mind-boggling peculiarity of the whole incident, he noticed everyone happened to be dressed in some shade of gold.

"Doc, my Eunice—she didn't. . ."

He forced a smile and tried to give what reassurance he could honestly offer. "The babe's already made her appearance."

"Boy or girl?" one of the large, hairy men asked.

"A girl, you dolt!" The other smacked him with a battered hat. "He said 'her,' so it's gotta be a girl!"

"And my Eunice? She's fairin' well?"

Well, he'd tried to avoid this. But he couldn't very well lie. "I can't say. My offer of help was refused." The admission galled him—a little because of his pride but mostly because he genuinely worried about that woman. Her niece wanted to treat her with—of all things—rust and bootleg rye whiskey.

"We'll see 'bout that!" The father shouldered through the crowd of children who spanned everything from diapered to desirable and opened the door. "Eunice, you let this here

17

sawbones come see to you and little Elsiebelle."

"It ain't been half an hour yet, so you jest turn tail and wait 'til me and Elvera are ready!"

Someone slammed the door, and Eric watched in disbelief as the other two men burst out laughing. "Shoulda knowed that'd happen," one said.

"You broke the rule," the other short, wiry one agreed.

A school-age, barefoot boy scratched a bony elbow and scrunched his sunburned nose. "Pa, what's a vera?"

The father glowered at them. "She done went and named my baby girl Elvera!"

"I swan that name's sorta pretty, Pa."

The scowl melted, and the huge man sat down on the porch step. He opened his arms, and a whole bunch of children pressed into him for a tangled hug. "Iff'n she's half as pretty as y'all, my heart's gonna bust."

Another redheaded woman came toward them from behind the barn. From the looks of her, she'd be having a child in four or five months. From the way she waddled at this early point of her carrying months, Eric knew this child had to have several brothers and sisters ahead of it. For now, that redhead had a knot of young children skipping at her heels and clinging to her skirt. "Did Eunice make me an aunt?"

A hundred times or so, I'd say, Eric thought.

"Aunt Lois! She had a Vera!"

Lois grinned and nodded. "Now ain't that the finest thang you ever heared? Johnna, yore old 'nuff to come on inside with me. The rest of you young'uns pay heed to what your pas tell you."

Things continued in that bizarre vein. The crowd parted to allow them access, then the door shut yet again—with both the doctor and father still left outside!

Eric marveled that this clan endured. They must be exceptionally hearty stock to survive the appalling medical "practices" he'd witnessed. The cabin had been tidy, and a quick glance around showed the ranch to be well kept. Surely that ought to be counted as a good sign. These folks wanted to succeed. They might kick a little, but when he demonstrated the advantages of the scientific advances, they'd progress into the modern age.

"Thanks for coming anyway, Doc." The young man he'd seen in town—Peter—extended a callused hand.

Eric shook it. "I'm glad no one used the ax."

Peter shook his head. "Uncle Hezzy'll never hear the end of that."

"I saw a perfectly good pair of scissors in there."

Confusion furrowed Peter's brow. "What do scissors have to do with anything? They're too puny to cut much pain."

"The ax was supposed to cut the pain," Eric deduced. He didn't know whether to be astonished by that nonsense or glad they hadn't used it to cut the cord.

Unaware of the doctor's thoughts, Peter nodded. "Only Uncle Hezzy lost the ax, and Aunt Eunice has a long memory when it comes to things like that. Bet he'll even let her name the next baby, too."

The door opened. Lois came back out. "Hezzy, go say howdy to yore new babe. The rest of you, take your turn, then come on over for supper. Got a big ol' mess of chicken an' dumplin's ready."

As the others crowded to go see the latest member of this enormous family, Polly exited the cabin. "Doctor, let's talk."

"Yeah, Doc." Lois beamed at him. "We'll fatten you up a mite and get to know you."

Eric shouldered through the throng and made it to Polly's

side. They'd mentioned Polly was a niece. No use insulting her—and especially not in front of family. He'd ruffled feathers, and as soon as he calmed her, they'd review Eunice's delivery. In the meantime, he refused to budge. "This little lady and I need to compare medical notes. I'm sure you all understand."

"We'll sit here on the porch." Polly lowered herself onto a bench. "That way, we'll be close to Eunice and Elvera."

Eric sat on the other end of the bench. "Absolutely."

"Then I'll jest send out some vittles for ye." Lois turned and headed into another cabin.

Eric's stomach rumbled. He figured he might as well have a quick supper and turn Polly into an ally. Then he'd go make sure Eunice and Elvera hadn't suffered any complications. A mouth-watering aroma filled the air, and he nodded his head as a young woman handed him a sizable bowl. "Thank you."

"Welcome." She blushed.

Polly accepted the other bowl and murmured her thanks. He'd said a quick prayer, but he waited until she finished her silent grace before taking a taste from his bowl. "This is excellent!"

"Lois would be pleased to send you home with a jar."

His sense of humor kicked in, so he muttered, "Eunice was ready to send me home in a jar."

Polly didn't bother to muffle her peal of laughter. "You caught her at a bad moment."

Her reaction pleased him. This young woman might be misguided, but she wasn't malicious. That boded well. "Soon as I'm done with this"—he lifted the spoon to his mouth and chose his words with exceeding care—"I'll go in and make sure matters are resolved."

Polly looked him directly in the eye. "Matters between you and Eunice, or medical ones?"

"Both," he answered succinctly. Several more MacPhersons ambled out of the cabin, but he stayed focused on her. "I took an oath—"

"I lernt 'bout that at school," a wiggly boy boasted. "It's the hip. . .the hip. . ." He strained, then jumped up and down. "The hippopotamus oath!"

"Nah, silly." One of the other older boys poked him. "It's the hypocrite's oath."

Amused, Eric said nothing.

Polly laughed again. The woman's laugh was light and free—sweet and nothing like the practiced giggles of the debutantes back East. "You're close, boys. It's the Hippocratic oath. Hippocrates was the father of medicine."

"Don't tell that to Hezzy," a beefy man moaned from the doorway. "He'll take a mind to name his next 'un 'Medicine' iff'n you do."

Though that observation set off a round of hoots, Eric knew better than to express an opinion. He lifted his bowl. "Good supper."

"Always welcome to come back for more, Doc." The man and children all ambled over to the supper cabin.

Eric then turned back to finish his explanation. "Polly, I meant every last word of the oath. It would be remiss of me to fail to render care."

"It would be remiss of you to fail to offer care. You did that." She took a bite of a dumpling, chewed it thoughtfully, then swallowed. "You're wearing what my mama calls a 'dig-in-the-heels look.' I suppose I could tell you everything's fine, but you're still going to march back in there."

He shrugged. "I won't pretend otherwise."

"Eunice is sure her milk will curdle if you upset her again." Nicely enough, Polly didn't even react when he choked on that little piece of information. Instead, she merely continued, "Perhaps it would be best if I eased you in and out real quick."

He gulped the last bite as he thumped his bowl onto the bench between them. "Good. Good."

She set aside her own half-eaten bowl and rose. Eric winced. In his urgency, he'd rushed her. It was all for a good cause. Only the dear Lord knew just what was happening with that mother in there.

"Stop scowling. I've had plenty." She tapped on the door, then opened it. "Aunt Tempy, Uncle Hezzy? Why don't you go eat supper? Doc and I will come sit with Eunice and the baby. I'm sure they'll be keeping you up all night."

"I don't need no doctorin'." Eunice lifted her head from the pillow and glowered at him.

"Doc wanted to see Elvera." Polly kept her tone light. "Let's let him estimate her weight." She slipped the baby from father to physician.

"Well, now!" Eric gently bounced the baby in his arms as a sense of awe swept over him. "Nice-sized. I'll have to take away a few ounces for this blanket, though. Someone quilted a fine one—warm."

"Eunice makes ev'ry young'un one whilst she's a-carryin'," her husband boasted.

"Well, I'd say she makes a fine blanket, but she makes an even prettier daughter. This one's eight pounds even. Let's take a look at those little fingers and toes." He needed to examine the babe, so he laid her on the bed next to her mama and opened the wrap.

"She's got long fingers. I'm thinkin' with our passel of young'uns, mayhap we should get a piany."

"Hmm. With those fingers, that would be possible. Wasn't that a mandolin I saw in the corner?" He lifted the gown and continued to confirm Elvera's health rated as superior.

" 'Tis mine," Tempy said. "And many of the children play it passingly well."

"If I don't put a stop to this, the next music is going to be you singing the praises of the MacPherson children." Polly plumped Eunice's pillow. "Aunt Tempy, Uncle Hezzy, go enjoy your supper."

"I reckon we will. You'll be jest fine here, Lambkin. Doc agrees with our Polly that Elvera's eight pounds, so he must know what he's about."

That had to be the most backhanded, ridiculous endorsement Eric had ever received. He didn't let on. Instead, he nodded. That action, he'd found, often rescued him.

He tucked the baby into Eunice's arms as the others departed, then deftly drew back the covers.

"Polly, if that there doc dares ta lift my hem, I aim to clobber him. Should you be a-holding my little Elvera?"

"The doctor can speak for himself." Polly's calm blue gaze rested on him.

"I'm able to assess the womb like this." He placed his hand over Eunice's gown. "It's firm, and that's good. Very good." Satisfied she couldn't be hemorrhaging, he covered her once again. "Mrs. MacPherson, I'm pleased you and your daughter are in the pink of health. Having thirteen children is quite an accomplishment."

"Yore a-tellin' me." She let out a raspy laugh. "All of us together got twenty-four. Lois and Obie got 'leven—soon to be twelve—but no need to mention that since you pr'bly took note on that fact. Tempy and Mike have nine."

The woman must not have had any schooling. Her arithmetic was faulty.

She lovingly traced the tiny whorls of the baby's hair. "We

done lost five when the diphtheria hit, and a few others jest winnowed away back to the bosom of Jesus when He took a mind to call 'em home."

"My condolences."

"He talks pretty, Polly." Eunice gave her niece a weary look.

"I venture it's more owed to him having a good heart than a glib tongue." Polly gave Eunice a sip of something. "Now you sleep. We'll be here."

We'll be here. Not I'll be here. Eric pulled up a chair and sat by the bed. Things were looking up. When he first got here, Polly told him a man had no place at a birthing. Now she'd accepted him.

Surely this little MacPherson woman had opened the door for him. If her loving but misguided family allowed him to treat them, then the rest of Reliable ought to follow suit. It was all working out so well—he'd asked the Lord to send him somewhere where he was needed. Now, more than ever, Eric knew he was in the center of God's will.

three

"Wake up, sleepyheads." Polly woke her cousins the next morning as she put down her gathering sack. She and Mama Lovejoy went gathering almost every morning—as much for the quiet time together as for the opportunity to harvest essential plants. Even though Uncle Mike had brought Polly home late last night, she hadn't been able to sleep in. As soon as the first rays of sun crept into the sky, her eyes always popped open.

"Polly," Laurel said from their bed up in the loft, "must you sound so cheerful this early?"

" 'This is the day the Lord hath made; I will rejoice and be glad in it.' "

April and Kate crawled out of the bed they shared and shimmied down the ladder in their ruffled nightgowns. Kate waggled a finger at her. "It's a good thing the Bible doesn't say anything about being jolly at night, because you'd use that as an excuse to wake us up, too!"

"It's our turn to make breakfast," April said. "Stop teasing her."

Laurel stayed in bed and began unwinding the rags from her hair. She managed to make rolling and unrolling those long tresses look so easy. It took her just a few minutes to accomplish it.

Polly unraveled her night braid, brushed her hair, and twisted it several times to form a bun at the back of her head. No matter where she stabbed in the hairpins, they didn't tame the wisps or keep the arrangement orderly. One last glance at Laurel made her give up. "I'm hopeless," she muttered.

April turned backward so Polly would help her with her stays. "Not too tight."

Polly tugged and tied, then gave her back a pat. Sweet April. She could cook, and her waistline tattled on all of the little tastes she took. "How about if I make coffee cake this morning?"

"I'll help you." April whirled around. "We'll bake bread, too."

Polly arched a brow. "Are you doing that for my sake or yours?"

Her cousins all laughed. Polly could follow instructions to formulate any elixir, unguent, or salve, but she couldn't follow a recipe if her life depended on it.

Yanking on a stocking, Kate mused, "I think it's because April wants to hear more about that new doctor."

"So what if I do?"

"April!" Polly gawked at her. "You're only sixteen."

"Plenty of girls marry when they're sixteen." April's chin lifted. "And—"

"And it's because they either don't have family to help them or the brains to know better." Polly shook her head. "Your daddy hasn't given you leave to even walk with a boy. What makes you think he'd let a doctor half again your age pay you court?"

Laurel stood at the mirror and neatly tied a bow at her throat. "You're simply too young and unsophisticated."

"And you aren't?" April half-shouted.

Polly held up a hand. "Whoa. We're all together here in this cabin. Remember our motto? 'God help us all.' I won't stand for squabbles. We're here to love and care for one another."

April's chin shook. "Sorry."

Laurel came over and settled her hand on April's arm. "I'm not setting my cap for the doctor. Don't think I'm trying to steal your man." Laurel sighed. "Truly, April, I'm eighteen and barely old enough myself, but I couldn't abide marrying a doctor."

"She couldn't wash the blood from his sleeves," Polly said succinctly. She then turned and glowered. "Kathryn Anne, don't you dare." In the midst of the conversation, Kate tried to wiggle into her dress without wearing her stays. Kate made a face, but she reached for the garment she hated.

"Let's go get breakfast," April muttered.

"I thought maybe I'd try Mrs. Dorsey's casserole recipe for lunch today," Laurel said as she headed toward the door. She waited until Kate was decent before opening it. "I want to perfect it for the next church supper. After all, the way to a man's heart is through his stomach."

"Then I'm going to be a spinster," Polly said as she tugged Kate along. At the moment, being a spinster didn't seem like such a dreadful fate. Trying to keep track of her cousins and sidetrack their wild plans had become a nonstop job. But a husband like that tall, handsome, growly voiced Doctor Walcott would make handling children more than worthwhile.

❧

Eric wiped the last dot of lather from his face, then cleaned his razor. A knock sounded.

"Breakfast in five minutes, Doctor."

"Thank you." He shrugged into his shirt and inhaled deeply to detect what the boardinghouse featured for breakfast. His cabin with the downstairs office wasn't available until the end of the month. Until then, he'd stay here. His bag and a crate of essential medicaments lay against the far wall, and it was awkward not to have an examining room. *It's just temporary. I chose to arrive early.*

What an arrival. He'd no more than stepped foot into the mercantile when a young man barreled through the door, shouting about a woman in labor and needing an ax. Eric mounted up and rode along to the MacPhersons. He'd returned late last evening and hadn't met any townsfolk yet. How many of Reliable township's inhabitants were hillbillies? Would they all cling to the misguided ways and silly notions he'd seen Polly employ yesterday?

The advertisement he'd responded to stated the town was a "thriving place near a metropolis." Well, San Francisco was a day away, but Eric wondered if their concept of thriving matched Polly's notion of medicine.

He didn't smell any particular aroma until he opened his door. "Mmm. Coffee."

A man exiting the room next to his chuckled. "Makes waking up worth it. I'm Bob Timpton." They shook hands.

"Eric Walcott."

As they tromped downstairs, Bob said, "No one was expecting you here yet."

"It took less time than expected to close matters back East." They sat at the table and waited until a gentleman at the head of the table said grace. As soon as folks started passing the platters and bowls, Eric asked, "Any recommendations on where I can buy a decent horse?"

"Chance Ranch," someone across the table and another two seats down said in unison.

"Fine horseflesh," Bob attested. "They'll give you a fair price. Livery can board your mount."

The owner of the boardinghouse leaned over his shoulder to fill his mug. "Dr. Walcott, I'm sure you aimed to pay a professional visit to the Chances, anyway."

"Is someone ill?"

"No, no." She continued to round the table, filling cups. "Lovejoy and Polly Chance live there. I'm sure you'll all be working together."

"Polly?" The bacon scraped his throat as he swallowed it too quickly. "She's not a MacPherson?"

"She's a Chance. They're loosely related. Not even kissing cousins." Last cup filled, the woman whisked off to the kitchen.

"So Polly wasn't merely helping out her aunt yesterday." Coffee churning in his stomach, Eric tried to digest this news. He didn't have to coax Polly into stepping aside to treat her family; he had to completely take away the business she and her mother ran. Quite literally, only God knew what they'd done to patients in the name of medicine. This was going to take finesse. Tact. Prayer. But Eric knew then and there he couldn't sit back and permit backwoods myths and folklore to be the basis for curing people in the modern age.

Times were changing. These people would, too—even if he had to nudge them. It was his duty, because he'd taken an oath. Nothing—and no one—would stop Eric Walcott from keeping that pledge. Not even some pretty little wheat-haired, wide-eyed, whiskey-dispensing girl.

❧

"Oh. Look at him!" April whispered to Polly at the water pump.

Polly cast a glance over her shoulder, then straightened up. "Hello, Doctor!"

"Hello." He cast a keen glance toward the main house, and for good cause. Perry kept letting out bloodcurdling screams. "Is everything okay?"

"Mama's fixing up Perry," Polly said. "He took a fall."

"I see." The doctor scanned toward the barn. "Are your men around?"

"Which ones?" April hefted a bucket.

Doc Walcott dismounted from a sorry-looking old nag. "Whoever is in charge of the horses."

"Uncle Gideon's in the main house." Polly lifted another bucket. "This way, please."

The doctor silently took both buckets from the girls and followed. Polly appreciated his manners. He'd not made a big deal out of helping with such an ordinary task, but simple things like that tattled about a man's character.

April scurried ahead and flung open the door. "We have a caller. It's the doctor."

"I don't want the doctor," Perry cried. "I want Auntie Lovejoy!"

Polly turned to the doctor. "Please don't take offense. Perry's a tad riled."

The doctor set down the buckets just inside the door and headed toward the noise. "What seems to be the problem?"

Mama turned to him, but she also held Perry's hand. "Nothing a few stitches won't solve. This little feller took a leap into the hayloft and didn't aim true."

Uncle Gideon held Perry on his lap and kept the towel wrapped about him so he couldn't squirm much. "Look at what Laurel has, Perry. You get to pick whatever color stitches you want."

Laurel held out a fistful of silk embroidery floss. "I brought lots of colors so you could choose whatever you like best."

"What are you putting on him?" Doctor Walcott's eyes narrowed as he watched Mama.

"Toothache plant." Mama stopped pressing ice to the gash and started to rub the flower against the edges. When Perry whimpered, she said in a loud whisper, "You're brave as a buccaneer, so I'm a-thinkin' mayhap black's the color for you."

"Ben had black." Even though Perry's lower lip trembled, it

now stuck out in a pout. "It looked like a big, fat woolly worm."

"Iff'n I make the X to mark the spot dead center, we'll all know 'tis like a treasure map."

Polly watched as Mama finished applying the toothache plant. The ice began numbing the cut; toothache would finish numbing it and act as an antiseptic. With so many children around, the family had the whole technique down to an art by now. Polly or Mama numbed and treated the wound while another adult kept hold of the child and others distracted him. Polly headed for the stove and brought over a pot of boiling water.

"I wanna treasure map," Perry sniffled.

"I'll make a fine one. No fair lookin' 'til I'm done, though. It's the rule."

Uncle Gideon pulled the towel tighter to hold his nephew immobile and cupped his hand around Perry's head. "Close your eyes. Kate will tell you a story, so you listen real good."

Kate started in with a swashbuckling story as Mama threaded the needle and dipped it and the floss into the boiling water. Doc Walcott hovered close. Though Polly would normally assist, she could tell the doctor itched to help out. All in all, it was probably a good idea for him to see up close just how skilled Mama was. That way, when he did surgery, he'd have the assurance that capable assistants were on hand. Polly took him over to the washstand. "If you scrub, you can clip for Mama."

He scrubbed thoroughly but with almost blinding speed, then went back to assist. His brows rose as he realized Mama was already half done with the sutures, but he picked up the scissors and started clipping the thread after the knot so Mama could continue on with the next stitch. He stepped back when it was all done.

"And so he sailed off toward the sunset," Kate finished.

Perry sniffled. "Can I look now?"

"Shore 'nuff cain," Mama said. "Lookie there at yore treasure map. 'Tis a cryin' shame to have to cover it up with a bandage, but we'll have to."

The little boy inspected the gash. "That's a map?"

"Here." Doc Walcott dipped the blunt end of a probe into a bottle of iodine. He painted along the suture line, then drew another streak perpendicular to the sutures. "We don't want anyone but our crew to know you have the treasure map, so here's what we're going to do. . . . North, south, east, and west. See? We made it a compass." He drew an odd shape around the boy's arm. It didn't escape Polly's notice that he managed to trace over the deeper scratches. "That's Hazard Island."

"Is it, Auntie Lovejoy?" Perry asked.

"Niver seen better." Mama smiled.

"Do I gotta have a bandage?"

"Absolutely." Doc Walcott smiled. "I'll put it on."

Perry stared at the doctor, then slowly shook his head. "Auntie Lovejoy and Polly take care of us when we get sick or hurted."

"I see." Doc nodded sagely. "Well, I came to see about buying a horse, so I'm glad the trip was still useful."

"We got lotta horses."

"Good." Doc smiled at Uncle Gideon. "Word has it you sell the best horses around."

"Daddy, he needs a horse badly," April said. She managed to sidle next to the doctor. "You should see what he rode in on!"

"My grandfather's horse isn't suited to this terrain. I hadn't realized there'd be such heavy riding, and she's too old. I'd like to turn her out to pasture. She served well, but the time has come to move ahead." Doc's explanation showed sense and compassion. Both fine qualities.

"What do you have in mind?" Uncle Gideon waited until Mama finished tying the bandage; then he ruffled Perry's hair and set him down. "We've horses aplenty."

"If possible, I'd like to get a young, even-tempered mount and pay lodging for the old mare to live out her days here."

"That must be hard to do," April cooed.

Polly wondered what had come over her cousin. Then again, she didn't. April was trying to flirt, and she was making a ninny of herself.

Doc shrugged. "Things serve a purpose. In life, new things come along. No reason not to trade up to something better."

Polly got a funny sensation in the pit of her stomach as he spoke. Then again, it might not be the words he used. Sometimes when she had a headache brewing, she got that same sick feeling. As soon as the men went outside to look at horses, Polly slipped away and took some feverfew, then returned to the kitchen and started making sandwiches. Soon the happy chatter around her made her wince. Pain streaked from her right temple to behind her ear. Within minutes, she set aside the knife and whispered to Mama, "I'm going to go lie down."

Mama frowned. "Yore pale as a new moon. You getting a sick headache again?"

"I took some feverfew."

"Aww, my Pollywog." Mama slid an arm around her waist and guided her toward the door. "Jest close yore eyes and cover them. Sun's bright as cain be. I'll lead you."

Polly stumbled along, and seconds later Mama stopped.

"Not again." Uncle Titus spoke in a low whisper. "C'mere." He lifted Polly and carried her to her cabin.

four

Eric exited the barn and surveyed the layout of the ranch. Several cabins formed three sides of a rectangle. Lush gardens abounded, and half a dozen picnic tables took up part of the yard. Clearly, several branches of the family tree still lived and worked together here.

Movement off to one side captured his attention. A dark-haired man carried Polly into a cabin. Her head rested on his shoulder—a rather romantic scene, especially at midday in the middle of a big family barnyard.

Maybe I haven't quite gotten things straight. Maybe she's married to one of these men. Good. She'll be too wrapped up in family matters to tromp around and play doctor much longer.

He tried to convince himself of that. After all, he'd just seen Lovejoy Chance rub a fresh flower all over a gaping wound. If it didn't fester, it would be due only to heavenly intervention and the iodine Eric had painted on after the sutures. These people were practicing medieval medicine in the modern age.

"Your saddle and tack look to be in good shape," Gideon said.

"Yes, they are. I'll just switch it over to that gelding."

"One of the boys'll do it after lunch." Gideon headed toward the picnic tables in the yard. "Come have a seat. We eat lunch in shifts. That way, work doesn't have to grind to a halt."

The man he'd seen carrying Polly just moments before approached them. Up close, he looked far older. *That could be good—he'll have a stabilizing influence on Polly.*

"Doc, Lovejoy asked if you could take a peek at Polly."

"Oh?"

"Yeah. My niece gets these rip-roarin' headaches. Come on of a sudden and lie her low for days."

"I see." Eric headed toward the cabin into which he'd seen the man carry Polly. Headaches were symptoms of several maladies, but from what the man just described, Polly probably suffered from migraines. Unfortunately, modern science hadn't yet found the cure for that dreadful malady.

Concerned for her, Eric almost reached the small porch before the words sank in. That man had called Polly his niece. They weren't lovebirds—they were just close kin. *If I want to see her married off, then why am I not sad at that news?*

Eric didn't dwell on that question. For now, he had a patient to treat. The second he stepped foot on the porch, the door opened and someone grabbed him and yanked him inside. The door whispered shut.

By way of excuse for the abrupt action, Lovejoy murmured, "Light troubles her."

He nodded as his eyes adjusted to the dim cabin. The place definitely belonged to women. It smelled of flowers and held white-painted furniture. A loft increased the space significantly, but his eyes narrowed as he realized no stairs led up to it. Surely no one in the clutches of a migraine ought to be climbing the slender ladder propped against the rail. Spotting something in the corner, Eric headed there.

"I made her a pallet." Lovejoy brushed past him and knelt. Stroking the cloth over Polly's forehead, she whispered, "Honey, Doc's here to see you."

Other than the fact that the corners of her mouth tightened, Polly gave no response. She made for a huddled ball of misery.

Eric knelt down and began by pushing a hairpin from the

pillow. Pesky, stupid things. If she had any more hiding in that bun she wore at her crown, they'd skewer her. Cradling the nape of her neck in one hand, he reached under her head and searched for more of the offending items. Masses of soft curls filled his hand.

"Thankee." Lovejoy took the pins from him. "I hadn't got 'round to that yet."

"Which side hurts?" he whispered.

Polly's lips moved silently. *Right.*

He turned her head that way. It seemed paradoxical that the pressure in the head caused this agony, but contact lessened the pain for many.

"Light and sound are troubling you. Are you nauseated?"

Yes, she mouthed.

Silently, he performed an examination. Pain darkened the blue of her eyes when he checked her pupils. He ruled out this being a sinus headache or allergy attack. Her hands shook and were cold when he checked her grip and pulse.

"She took feverfew," Lovejoy said.

"Good." That fact surprised him. He'd have prescribed that selfsame remedy. "How long ago?"

" 'Bout fifteen minutes or so. Often as not, it doesn't make a difference."

"Exceptionally strong coffee sometimes works."

"No," Polly moaned.

From the sick way she swallowed, Eric surmised Polly had tried coffee to cure the headache before and hadn't managed to keep it down. "Laudanum." He doubted it would do more than help her sleep through the pain, but that would count as a blessing.

"Makes her sick as cain be." Lovejoy shook her head. "Niver give her that stuff. It makes things worse 'stead of better."

Eric filed that piece of information away in the back of his mind. Those facts mattered, and he figured he'd treat Polly for various reasons in the coming years. In the past, he knew some doctors who carried their bags no matter where they went. He'd considered it overkill. Now he rethought his stance as he hit the end of his possible treatments. Careful to pitch his voice low, he asked Lovejoy, "Do you have oil of peppermint?"

"Shorely do." She slipped off.

Eric folded the cold compress and replaced it over Polly's eyes. Just yesterday, she'd been a tigress. Now she'd become helpless as a kitten. The tigress would inevitably cause him many annoyances, but he'd rather have her back.

Lovejoy handed him a small glass jar. "Niver used this for the headache. Hit's good for stomach ailments." Other than her colorfully archaic hill-country words, she spoke much like Polly. Their tone carried confidence and comfort. Last evening, after Eunice had fallen asleep, Polly's volume dropped to this same hushed whisper that barely stirred the air.

I've never used it to treat a headache, either. I recall my grandmother borrowing it for a maid, but I'm not about to confess that. They need to have confidence in this. Sometimes it's not the treatment but just the belief that it will work. Eric nodded to Lovejoy. "Oil of peppermint is known to work for both stomach ache and headache."

"You got a fine touch. The carin' shows."

The candy-sweet fragrance of peppermint filled the air as he uncapped the bottle. Eric removed the compress only long enough to rub oil on Polly's temples and forehead. The texture of her skin was soft as her hair, but tension pulled it taut. He could literally feel the ache. Eric capped the bottle, set it aside, and murmured, "Do you want anything, Polly?"

No.

"Precious Lord Jesus, hold my Polly." Lovejoy smoothed the blankets and continued to pray under her breath.

Prayer. On that, they agreed.

❧

Polly closed her Bible and took another sip of tea. Though the migraine finally eased off last night, her stomach still felt tipsy. Oftentimes after a headache, her stomach stayed unsettled for a day or so—but she secretly wondered if part of it might be butterflies. After all, Dr. Walcott hadn't just checked in on her the day he was here buying a horse. He'd also come back again late this morning.

"So now that you're done with devotions, tell me," Kate said as she sat down beside Polly and leaned close, "wasn't it thrilling to have the doctor come pay you a visit?"

"It was a medical call, not a visit," Polly replied.

"Of course it was," Laurel agreed, far too fast. Her huge smile and the tightness at the corners of that smile labeled her as a patent liar. "I'm sure if it were any of the boys who complained of a sick headache, Dr. Walcott would have been just as concerned and would have taken their hand in his for minutes on end."

"He was taking Polly's pulse," April snapped.

He had taken her pulse for a long while. Just the memory set those butterflies into flurries again. Steadying herself with a deep breath, Polly warned herself, *Don't be a fool and imagine something stupid. It was merely professional concern.* Long ago Mama taught her to be careful about this very issue—folks felt grateful and vulnerable when sick and newly healed. Sometimes they mixed up the appreciation with attraction. *He came for my headache, not for me,* Polly told herself firmly. Then she looked at her cousins and said that very thing.

"Are you coming to supper?" Laurel stood by the stove,

exchanging the sadirons so she could press their Sunday dresses.

"I think I'll stay here." The notion of some quiet time felt good. Polly had a lot of thinking and praying to do.

"I'm thinking perhaps I ought to skip supper myself," Laurel confessed. "I want to be able to cinch in my waist tomorrow."

"You don't need to," Polly said. "A man could span your waist with his hands."

"I have to keep it that way."

"Oh, stop being so vain," April moped. "Every man in the county is after you. It's not as if you can't capture whomever you set out to attract."

"I already know who I want." Laurel giggled. "I'm trying to keep his attention."

"You won't see him 'til tomorrow at church," April said. She handed the hairbrush off to Kate and started to towel her wet hair. "And if you help me put my hair up in rags tonight, I'll even polish your shoes."

"I'd help you curl your hair anyway." Laurel leaned forward and whispered loudly to Polly, "I think she's still hoping to have the new doctor take notice of her."

April headed out the door. "So what if I am?" She shut the door before her cousins could react.

"What got into her?" Kate set down the hairbrush and took up her mending. Awkwardly mending a hole in her petticoat, she said, "We're both sixteen, and I'm smart enough to know a woman doesn't chase a man. Why doesn't she? Polly, you'd better sit her down and talk sense into her."

"That's Aunt Miriam's place. I'll give April my opinion if she asks, and when we're around the doctor, I'll try to help her so she doesn't make a ninny of herself."

"Oh, she's sure to do that. Ouch!" Kate jerked back her

hand, dropped the mending, and popped her finger into her mouth.

Polly sighed. "If she brings up the topic, we need to be direct but gentle. Her feelings are running high. Honesty is essential, and we'd be failing her if we pretended it would be a sound match, but I don't want either of you teasing her. If you do, she'll dig in her heels, and it'll be a mess."

Laurel swept the iron back and forth, navigating ruffles with great skill. "Polly, why don't you set your cap for the doctor? You'd make a fine pair, I'm sure."

"I agree!" Kate bravely picked up the needle once again. "Think of all the help you could give one another."

"When the time comes for me to marry, I want a man who loves me as a wife—not someone who's looking to get a nurse for free."

"Of course you do," Laurel said. "I was just trying to point out that the two of you have a lot in common. That always makes for a happy home."

"We barely know each other. Snap judgments like that are bound to be fraught with danger. To my way of thinking, the home we need to concern ourselves with is this one. One of us chasing after a man is one too many."

"Well, I'm just saying you need to keep your eyes open to the men God puts in your life." Laurel set down the iron, lifted her midnight blue gown from the ironing board, and gave it a pleased shake. As she pretended to waltz across the plank floor, she shot Polly a coy glance. "I don't intend to be mean, but you're getting old."

"Old?" Polly gave her cousin an offended look.

"Now don't get all fussy on me. I'm trying hard to make sure you'll be happy in the future."

"Pastor Abe always tells us not to worry about tomorrow."

Laurel hung her dress in the wardrobe. "All right. So let's look at that entire verse in Philippians 4: 'Be careful for nothing; but in every thing by prayer and supplication with thanksgiving let your requests be made known unto God.' I'm saying we need to be praying about a husband for you."

"Oh, no," Polly heaved an impatient breath. "Keep going. Verse 7: 'And the peace of God, which passeth all understanding, shall keep your hearts and minds through Christ Jesus.' I've a peace about this. When the time comes, the man will come."

"I agree." Laurel gave her a sweet smile, then singsonged, "Verse 8: 'Finally, brethren, whatsoever things are true, whatsoever things are honest, whatsoever things are just, whatsoever things are pure, whatsoever things are lovely, whatsoever things are of good report; if there be any virtue, and if there be any praise, think on these things.' I'm telling you it's time for you to think on those things."

"What I'm thinking about is we're going to have a bunch of hungry Chances banging on our door if we don't go to supper!"

"Oh, so you're going now?" Kate hopped up.

Polly rubbed her forehead. "Why not?"

Polly thought she'd managed to hold her own with Laurel's matchmaking conversation until they cleaned up after supper. Laurel dropped a handful of silverware into the sink. "Aunt Lovejoy, it occurs to me that we ought to invite the new doctor to Sunday supper."

"There's a right fine notion." Mama Lovejoy bobbed her head. "Poor feller's on his lonesome. Hope he'll come to worship. Mayhap Dan'l can give him the invite."

"Yes. That's a wonderful idea," Laurel enthused. She shot Polly a sideways glance and grinned.

"Man likely doesn't know a soul. He jest moved here."

"That's true." Laurel's tone set Polly's nerves jangling. "It's the way of the world for all of us to grow up and move on. Why, one of these days, Polly will marry and move away. Most of us will—though not as soon."

Polly tamped down the urge to serve Laurel a secret little kick.

Mama turned to her. "You got yore eye on somebody, Polly-mine?"

"When I fall in love, you'll be the first to know."

Dread snaked through Polly. She knew that look in Mama's eyes. It said, *This topic isn't over yet.* Just as soon as dishes were finished, Mama walked outside and steered her off to the side. "So what's this 'bout you marryin' up and movin' on?"

"Laurel's being silly. She's wanting someone to pay court to her, and I think she's afraid I'm supposed to be married first."

Mama nodded sagely. She peeled bark from an oak with economical movements for a few seconds, then cast away the shreds. "What do you think?"

"The bark was too damp."

"I'm not askin' 'bout the bark, and well you know it."

Polly smiled. "I'm in no hurry to get married. All three of the girls could marry before me, and I wouldn't be upset. You always told me to wait for the man who set my heart afire. Until he comes along and kindles the flame, I'm content to wait."

five

"Hey, Doc?" A slick-looking man strode into the boarding-house. "How 'bout you grab your bag and follow me?"

"Jake's got trouble at the saloon again," one of the men muttered. He gave Eric a telling look.

"Go on ahead," Bob said. "I'll ask them to keep some supper in the warmer for you."

"Thanks." Eric hastened upstairs, grabbed his bag, and followed the saloon keeper. "What sort of difficulty will I be treating?"

"You'll see."

The brightness of the street gave way to the dank atmosphere of the saloon. Eric followed Jake up the crimson-carpeted stairs. Jake motioned him into a room, then shut the door. A painted woman sat by an iron bed, murmuring softly to a sweat-soaked younger girl who was curled up tightly on her side. She looked up at him, spied his bag, and sighed.

"Jake found out she was carryin'. He gave her something, and now she's crampin' something fierce. No doubt, she'll lose the babe, but she's in a bad way. I told Jake to fetch your help, or we'd lose her, too."

Everything within Eric revolted. Just yesterday, he'd wanted to try to pull a mother and child through, and he'd been rebuffed. Now his first case was to salvage the life of a soiled dove whose child was not to be. *Lord, why?*

He set down his bag and rolled up his sleeves.

❧

"Gideon, I thought you invited the doctor to church," Aunt

Miriam said after the service.

"I did." Uncle Gideon helped Aunt Miriam into the buck-board, then lifted in their youngest sons.

"I heard him," Polly heard Daddy say as he lifted Mama Lovejoy in. He then swiped little Troy from Alisa, gave him to Mama, and lifted Alisa in.

Mama gave Aunt Daisy a look that bordered on frazzled. "But neither of them thought to ask the man to supper."

Daddy and Uncle Gideon didn't look the least bit chastened. Uncle Gideon leaned over and kissed Aunt Miriam's temple. "Everyone for miles around knows they're always welcome at our table."

"Everyone for miles around," Aunt Alisa pointed out, "has lived here for years. The doctor is new."

"Supper or not, it still woulda been nice for him to show up and let us know if he's happy with that new gelding," Calvin grumbled. "He's had it a few days now. I spent a lot of time taming and training that mount."

"It would have been nice to have the doctor come for worship," Aunt Miriam corrected her son.

"There was a time I didn't want to worship, either," Aunt Delilah confessed.

As the family chattered and loaded the smaller children into the buckboard, Kate, Laurel, and April all piled into the MacPhersons' rig. Polly still hadn't decided where she'd spend her Sunday afternoon. The notion of having the cabin to herself held some appeal. She didn't regret inviting the girls to move in with her, but the continual chatter when she was accustomed to silence and precious solitude did wear on her some of the time—especially when she suffered the aftermath of a migraine.

Complicating the matter even more, Kate and Laurel

managed to pair her up with the doctor in their conversations. April bristled over that fact until Polly finally sat up in bed last night and told them all to stop acting like a flock of gossipy, pecky hens. They'd apologized to one another, said a bedtime prayer, and slipped off to sleep.

Only Polly hadn't slept. *If I go home, I can be alone—even take a nap—without anyone bothering me.*

Uncle Bryce mounted his sorrel gelding and nosed him toward Polly. He reached a hand toward her. "Ride with me."

She rode pillion. None of the other girls did—they always rode ahead of a man on his horse, but Mama Lovejoy always rode pillion with Daddy, and Polly followed her example.

The older cousins and men rode horses to and from worship; the women and smaller children took two buckboards. Only now Bryce didn't take the usual path back to the ranch. He turned south and rode along the fence.

"Gotta talk," he finally said.

"What's on your mind?"

He squinted ahead and cleared his throat. "If you plan to meet with the doc or work with him, make sure your ma's with you."

"Is there a problem?"

"Might be."

Polly poked him. "Stop being so cryptic."

"I don't ask you 'bout the calls you pay on folks and what ails them."

"That's because they deserve their dignity and privacy. What does that have to do with the doctor?"

Uncle Bryce heaved a sigh. "Do you have to be so difficult?"

She laughed. "When haven't I been difficult?"

He chuckled. "You got a point there."

Polly waited. He didn't say anything more, so she prodded, "Well?"

"Can't tell you how I know what I know. I just know it."

"Okay, Uncle Bryce, so what do you know?"

"Doc spent half the night at the Nugget." He paused and tacked on, "He wasn't downstairs."

"I see."

Her uncle turned in the saddle and gave her a sour look. "I don't want you around that man."

"This isn't like you, Uncle Bryce. You don't make snap judgments."

"I'm not leaping to any conclusions. I know what I know, and I've told you as much as you need to know. I'm keepin' this just 'tween the both of us because I won't go blackening a man's name—but I'm not going to have your reputation sullied by association."

Polly took a deep breath and let it out slowly. "I'll do my best."

He nodded, then turned toward home.

They'd traveled about fifty yards when she tugged on his shirt. "Stop here. I'll gather some of this lupine as an excuse for us to have come by this way."

"We just left church—do I have to remind you that it's Sunday?"

Polly wasn't sure if he meant that she'd be walking a fine line in regard to being truthful or if he referred to the fact that unless a dire need for a particular herb existed, gathering on Sunday simply wasn't done. "I won't get in trouble. We need fresh flowers on the tables."

"Next thing you'll tell me is that you have your bag with you."

She laughed. Polly rarely went anywhere without her gathering knife or a bag to collect the plants, bark, or twigs that caught her fancy.

"That sounded like a guilty laugh."

Polly slid off the horse. "Turn your head." He muttered something under his breath, but he dismounted and complied. Polly yanked up the right side of her skirts and bent down to take the knife from the small sheath she'd buckled atop her ankle boots.

"Are you going to take all day? I'm hungry."

"You could help me."

Uncle Bryce turned around and let out a snort.

"Then make yourself useful and hang on to this." Polly handed him the bag, which he held open. In a few short minutes, she cut checkerbloom, lupine, and hound's-tongue. "There. That ought to do."

"Good. Let's go."

"Wait." Polly impulsively gave her uncle a hug. He was the youngest of her uncles and the last to get married. Aunt Miriam said he'd taken a special shine to Polly from way back, but the year diphtheria took his little stepson Jamie and her sister Ginny Mae, they'd mourned and comforted one another. Often she thought of him as being more like a cousin than an uncle. More than once, he'd stood up for her when the boys didn't understand why she was different. Bringing her out here for this conversation was another example of how he cared. "Thank you. I'll be mindful of what you told me."

He nodded. "You do that."

⁂

Much to Eric's regret, he'd slept straight through the church bells chiming. He'd been up late into the night tending that soiled dove and nearly lost her. It wasn't until the wee hours of the morning that she stabilized.

During his hours at the bordello, he'd managed to pass the word to the older painted woman that he had connections. In the future, if one of the "girls" found herself "in trouble," he could send her away where she'd be placed with a family and leave the baby for adoption. To his relief, she'd promised to whisper that possibility to everyone.

But his heart still weighed heavy. Wanting time alone with the Lord this morning, he'd grabbed his Bible and walked out of town. This spot seemed perfect for devotions—serene, beautiful, private. Unfortunately, he'd barely opened the Word when the couple rode by. He recognized Polly at once. He'd not yet seen the man before.

Unwilling to be present at a tryst, Eric closed his Bible and rose to leave. For some reason, he couldn't quite set his feet in motion. To his surprise, the couple didn't linger at all. Less than five minutes after they rode up, they rode off again. Judging from the hug, they were probably courting.

A smile chased across Eric's face. The day he'd bought his horse, he'd determined if Polly married, she'd have her hands full with helping her husband and rearing children. An older husband would be especially good for her—settle her down. And she'd looked at that man with a lot of tenderness.

In the short time he'd spent with her, Eric determined Polly was generous, gentle, and exceedingly kind. The man who married her would be getting a gem. Never before had he felt the emotion, but Eric diagnosed it immediately: He felt jealous of whoever that man was.

That's ridiculous. I'm glad. He and Polly will court, marry, and she'll be too busy to give me any grief. In the meantime, I'm going to have to cope with her trying to dally with my patients. He had a feeling that interim would be fraught with tension.

"Tincture of time," he said to himself. In medical school, one of his professors had said many ailments required little intervention but rather the "tincture of time" to be resolved. Well, in this situation, a short, sweet courtship and a trip to the altar would be his prescription for that young lady.

Eric sat down, opened his Bible again, and read Psalm 133: *"Behold, how good and how pleasant it is for brethren to dwell together in unity! It is like the precious ointment upon the head, that ran down upon the beard, even Aaron's beard: that went down to the skirts of his garments; as the dew of Hermon, and as the dew that descended upon the mountains of Zion: for there the* LORD *commanded the blessing, even life for evermore."*

Such a short chapter—but those three verses spoke volumes to him. Eric scanned them again and thought about how the Lord was faithful to speak through His Word.

Eric wanted to live in unity here—to be part of this place and help his brothers and sisters in Christ. The Chance men had already invited him to church and sold him a horse for a more than fair price. The folks at the boardinghouse welcomed him warmly. Mrs. White at the mercantile seemed pleasant enough. "The only fly in my ointment is that girl. God willing and tincture of time. . ."

Eric rose. Though he'd missed worshiping at church today, he'd still met with God. He ambled back toward the road. When he reached it, he looked in the direction opposite the town. A white clapboard building stood a ways off. He'd passed it that day he'd ridden out to the MacPherson place to offer his assistance with the birthing. The large size of the church had astonished him that day—but after he'd witnessed the size of the MacPherson clan, it made sense. The mayor hadn't been exaggerating when he wrote that the town was "thriving."

Eric walked back to town, dropped off his Bible, then went to see Kitty. He'd told the older woman to send for him if any complications arose during the night. Though no one came, Eric wanted to be sure the girl was all right. He gave a fleeting thought to slipping into the Nugget from the back door. Then again, that would give the appearance that he had something to hide. Instead, he walked through the bat-wing doors and headed straight up the stairs. The medical bag in his hand should provide answers to any questions the good folks of town might have about him frequenting such a place.

❧

"Outstanding medical supplies," Eric complimented Mrs. White two days later as he paid for Vaseline and five yards of soft, snowy cotton.

"I'm happy to order whatever you require." Mrs. White wrapped his purchase in brown paper. "Though from all the supplies I saw them unloading at your new place, it challenges me to think you might need anything more."

"My research showed the town didn't have a pharmacy. It seemed prudent to stock up on essentials. I thought it silly to pack material for bandages and slings when the mercantile would undoubtedly have a supply."

"I keep this particular bolt just for medical purposes." She ran her hand across the fabric to smooth it, then rolled unbleached muslin around it a few times to keep it sanitary.

Eric took note of how she minded such an important detail. "You can be sure I'll buy more."

She smiled. "Whenever you need it, let me know. I keep it in the back room."

"Excellent." He tucked the package under his arm and left. It was just a short walk down the street to his office. He'd officially take possession of the place today, but when his freight wagon pulled up late last evening, the town lawyer permitted the bullwhacker to dump all of the doctor's possessions in the just-vacated cabin. Even then, the lawyer declared that at 10:00 a.m. sharp, he'd give Eric the keys—and not a breath before.

Eric didn't desperately need the cotton or Vaseline. He'd

restlessly walked down the boardwalk and ended up in the mercantile. Buying those paltry items gave him an excuse to waste time.

From what he'd seen last night, the building he'd occupy and turn into his office and abode left much to be desired. A single large room made up the entire downstairs, and the sink at the rear had no pump for running water. A pair of support beams stood at awkward places in the middle of the room. The upstairs consisted of two modest-sized rooms.

His priority had to be simply getting things arranged in such a way that he could practice medicine. All other aspects of the move would fall into place in the passage of time.

Thump. "Ouch!"

Eric frowned at the sound coming from his place. He pushed open the already ajar door.

six

"Mornin', Doc." Daniel Chance stood by the closest boxes. He jerked his chin toward the hook on the wall to his right. "Your keys are over yonder."

"I see. Is everyone all right? Did you need assistance?"

Daniel chortled. "Doc, we're all right as rain. From the looks of it, you're the one who needs help."

"I do have a lot of work ahead of me."

"Hey, Uncle Dan," someone called from the head of the stairs, "want us to bring anything else up?"

Dan gave Eric a questioning look.

Eric looked around. "Perhaps my books. I can't have the boxes lying around down here, but I use my references heavily."

"Couple of shelves would be handy."

Three strapping Chance boys stomped down the stairs. Eric took one look and felt a flash of inspiration. "Would you mind carrying over a bookshelf if I buy one over at the mercantile?"

"Dan," someone said from the doorway, "I bought that metal mesh for the women. Got extra—looks good for keeping flies out the windows!"

"Titus, come meet the doc. Doc, this is one of my brothers, Titus. Titus, Doc Walcott."

Eric shook the man's hand. "Pleased to meet you. Back East, they've been stretching the mesh in frames and using them as doors. Nice ventilation in the heat of the summer."

Daniel chortled. "Titus, you'd better track back over to the mercantile and buy up whatever Mrs. White has."

"Not until I buy some first," Eric claimed. He looked around and winced. "Forget that. Take it all. I have plenty of other projects to do first to bring this place up to snuff."

"Like what?" one of the boys asked.

"A wall over there at that post." Eric waved toward the back. "And another perpendicular to it to divide the room up to this other post. A big T-shape will chop it into three sections. Shelves, cabinets, a pump at the sink. . ."

"Caleb and Calvin, did you hear that?" Daniel asked.

"Yes."

Titus and Daniel exchanged a look. Titus looked to the tallest boy. "Tanner, you go fetch Peter, Matt, and Mark. I'm sure the MacPhersons'll spare them. Swing by home and get the tools. We'll have them ready."

"Sure, Dad!" Tanner took off.

Feeling as if they'd committed him to something but not knowing exactly what it entailed or what it would cost, Eric held up a hand. "Hang on here." In the light of day, seeing the true condition of the place, Eric knew he desperately needed this help. On the other hand, he didn't want these men to feel he—or they—betrayed their women when Eric divested them of their "healing" careers.

"No need to thank us, Doc. We're just being neighborly." Titus nodded his head and walked straight out the door.

Daniel smacked his thigh and looked at his nephews. "Two hours. By then, you'd better have it framed." He strode out.

Caleb—or was it Calvin?—asked, "You got a yardstick 'round here somewhere?"

"Probably."

"Never mind," the other said. "I'll just pace if off." He walked heel to toe between the posts and counted his steps. "Doc, I need paper or a slate. Which walls did you want shelves on, and how deep do you want 'em?"

Eric dug out a pencil and a sheet of foolscap. He quickly drew an outline of the room. "Here's what I had in mind. This area back here will be for washing and sterilizing."

"You gonna cook any meals on the stove?"

"Not many." Eric made a face. "I'll end up having to doctor myself if I do."

The young men found his admission hilarious.

He tapped the left side of the remaining rectangle. "This will be my treatment room."

"So you'll need that big old table there to do examinations."

"Exactly." Eric felt a surge of energy. He'd planned on it taking awhile to establish himself and whip this place into shape. All of a sudden, God had opened an opportunity. Enthusiastically drawing a line between the posts to form a T-shape of walls in the room, he said, "Putting a wall here will create a waiting room and my office."

The boys looked around. "Is there a desk in here somewhere?"

"Back in that far corner, behind the crates." Eric looked at the two young men. "Let's set out a plan and budget."

"We got the plan now, Doc. Tanner's impatient, and we have framing to do. Cal and I'll go get the lumber from the feed store. Details will have to wait."

❧

Chances never do things by halves. Once we get going, we always go overboard, Polly thought as Tanner lifted her into the buckboard. The family tradition started when Uncle Gideon held a cabin raising for Aunt Miriam when she came to help rear Polly and her little sister. What was supposed to be one cabin turned into three that day.

Daddy and Uncle Titus had taken three of the boys to town this morning to help the doc move in his furniture. The project sort of mushroomed from there. Uncle Titus came home and said the doctor needed more help. Fifteen minutes later when Tanner came by, tools weren't all that filled the buckboard.

"Wait! I want to come, too!" April galloped up.

Polly winced. It wasn't her place to say no, but having April there would complicate matters. The girl had stars in her eyes over the doctor and couldn't see reason.

"Aw, April." Mama Lovejoy slipped her arm around April's shoulders. "My heart's set on pie tonight, and my back's painin' me too much to make crust. Nobody makes a finer pie than you. Won't you stay and holp?"

April's smile wobbled, then lifted. She slid her arm around Mama's waist and rubbed her back. "Of course I will."

Dear, sweet April. Polly knew this qualified as a huge sacrifice for her, but she didn't hesitate. She put Mama ahead of herself. Mama had been kicked by a horse last year and still suffered from it. The whole family pitched in to take over the heavy things whenever Mama took a mind to do too much. It was rare for Mama to ever admit weakness.

Polly smiled at her cousin. "Thank you, April. Thank you so much."

April continued to rub Mama's back. "Without all of you underfoot, we'll turn this place into a bakery."

"We'll be sure to come back for that," Aunt Delilah declared. "I guess we're off, then."

Once the buckboard traveled far enough from April to keep her from overhearing the conversation, Aunt Delilah turned to Polly. "Don't for one moment think we haven't noticed April mooning over the doctor. Nearly every girl fancies herself in love with a man and makes a nuisance of herself until she comes to her senses. We're counting on you girls to talk sense into her in that cabin of yours."

"We're doing our best," Polly said.

"Not that it shows," Laurel tacked on. "Honestly, Mama, I wouldn't blame the doctor if he got annoyed and told her to go play in the schoolyard."

"He's a gentleman. A gentleman wouldn't do such a thing. If he's got any common sense, he simply ignores the situation until the young lady decides to cast her affection elsewhere."

"If she doesn't cast it somewhere soon, I'm going to be tempted to cast her out the window," Kate said. "There I am, trying to sleep, and she swipes my pillow and asks me if I think she ought to take up embroidery so she can put her initials and his on a pair of pillow slips!"

Aunt Delilah hid her laugh with a cough. "This is far more serious than I thought if April is considering picking up a needle. The girl does magic with a rolling pin, but she's deadly with a needle!"

"Maybe you could have Aunt Miriam speak with her," Polly suggested. She couldn't be sure whether her aunt nodded in agreement or if it was just the bumpy road that made Aunt Delilah's head bounce up and down.

Oh, and the road did need work after all the spring rains. The women, tools, and supplies rattled in the buckboard on the way to town. Uncle Titus said the doctor's place looked filthy as a pigpen, so buckets, rags, and plenty of lye soap rested in a crate next to a good supply of food.

Aunt Delilah jostled against Polly and decided, "First off, you girls go on upstairs and scour it while I tend the kitchen. We're not taking a morsel of food into the place until it's spic and span. Then, Polly, while you unload the food, Laurel and Kate can measure the windows. I'll go to the mercantile and decide on paint and material for curtains."

Tanner called over, "Doc might want Polly to help him decide on where to put the medical supplies. He has crates of them."

"It'll be a pleasure to help him. I'd like to see what's new, and I can offer him some of our herbs." As soon as the doctor set up his office, folks would feel comfortable about seeking his help—maybe not at birthings but for other matters. That would be wonderful.

"Polly," Kate asked, "are you worried about Doc taking away patients?"

"Not at all. Mama and I are excited he's come. There's so much we haven't been able to do. Having him here for surgery and such will be a blessing. There's far too much for us to handle, and Mama's happier doing gathering and helping children than anything else. She just doesn't like me treating the men."

"None of us do." Aunt Delilah jounced along with them. "It's one thing for an older, married woman to work on men, but you're still a young lady."

"I'm sure some of those patients will seek out Dr. Walcott's care. You know me—I'm happiest delivering babies, and there isn't a man in the world who's going to need me to midwife him!"

Jars and bowls rattled. "Peter MacPherson, you'd better drive more smoothly," Aunt Delilah warned, "or lunch will be ruined."

❧

"Took you long enough," Calvin greeted them as he swept Laurel from the buckboard.

"Don't complain, or you won't eat." She moved to the side.

Polly winked at Laurel. Only she could say something that bossy and still sound charming.

"No eating until the job's done," Aunt Delilah declared as Tanner helped her down from the back of the buckboard.

"What job?" Bob Timpton asked from the boardwalk.

"We're just helping the doc set up," Tanner said.

"I'd offer to help, but—"

"Thanks," Calvin said as he looked at the family ganged around him, "but we have it handled."

While the men spoke, Polly rummaged through the cleaning supplies. She couldn't recall having brought any stove polish.

"Let me help you down."

The doctor's deep voice startled her. Her head jerked up. "Oh. Yes, well, thank you."

He'd rolled up his shirtsleeves, and the muscles in his forearms flexed as he curled his hands around her waist. The sight made her go breathless. *Dear me, I'm going giddy over nothing. I'm worse than April.*

"Here we go." He had her on the ground in just a second.

"Thank you," she said again. Realizing she'd thanked him twice, Polly blurted out something—anything—to divert his attention from that stupidity. "Your shirt is white. It's going to get dirty."

"All my shirts are white." He released his hold on her. "And I daresay dirt washes out more easily than blood."

"True."

"What can I carry in?"

Minutes later Laurel, Kate, and Polly all had kerchiefs over their hair, smudges on their faces, and dirt on their skirts. Polly missed April. The four of them always worked as a team, and it felt odd to have her gone. She'd stayed behind willingly, and Polly strained to think of a way she could show April her special appreciation for why she hadn't come today. Perhaps she could press flowers to make her a little toilette water or scent some glycerin soap. April loved lavender and lemon verbena. Either would be a nice little thank-you.

"I declare." Laurel's moan jarred Polly from her musings. "I can't imagine how anyone could live in such squalor."

Kate vigorously brushed grime from the window frame. "At least the men had the presence of mind to leave most of the stuff downstairs. I can't imagine trying to wash down all of this with a bed in the middle of the muddle."

"Middle of the muddle," Laurel singsonged back. "I like that. It's fun to say."

"I've never been in here before." Polly continued to wipe down the wall. "I'm glad it's plastered. It ought to clean up well."

"What color do you think we ought to paint it?" Kate nudged a clump of dusty old draperies.

"I don't know," the doctor said from the doorway. "I hadn't thought that far ahead. My planning went only so far as setting up my surgery."

"Since the walls will be clean and nothing's in here, it's an ideal time to go ahead and paint." Polly looked at him. "So do you have any preferences?"

"Do you?" he echoed back.

"Her favorite color is green," Laurel said.

"Green sounds like a fine color. Your aunt is downstairs attacking my oven. I—"

Laurel let out a peal of laughter. "Take my advice and don't go near her. You're liable to be conscripted into doing some of the dirty work."

"It's my place. I ought to." He shook his head. "The army needs to hire her. In less than three minutes, she had seven grown men dusting down the ceiling."

The window screeched as Polly finally forced it open. "Do you think it's funny that they cooperate, or are you amused because we'll have sawdust all over by the end of the day?"

"The former shows family spirit. I'm impressed. It's the latter." He bent down to take the draperies from Polly.

Polly watched as he looked down before tossing the dusty bundle out of the room. When he turned around, she informed him, "The dirt is old. Sawdust is fresh."

He gave her a wary look. "I see."

Polly nodded sagely, but she couldn't hide the laughter in her voice. "That's what my uncle Paul told Aunt Delilah when they added onto their cabin."

Doc chortled. "That explains why he was the first one to start cleaning."

Kate tossed down her scrub brush. "I, for one, am going downstairs. This is a sight never to be missed—Chance men doing housework!"

Laurel and Kate ran downstairs. Doc lifted a brow in silent query.

"My first memories are of Daddy and my uncles doing housework."

"Is that so?"

"Mother died soon after the birth of my sister." Polly turned to the side and resumed work. "Aunt Miriam is the first woman I remember, and from all accounts, the. . .um. . .housekeeping the Chance men had been doing wasn't exactly to standard."

"I see. So which of the girls is your sister?"

Her hand halted. "Ginny Mae passed on from diphtheria when she was ten."

"My condolences."

"Hey, Doc!" someone shouted from down below.

Doc gave her a look filled with compassion and apology, then turned and headed downstairs. "Yes?"

A moment later, hearty guffaws filled the air. Polly could pick out Dr. Walcott's laughter.

෴

Food overflowed Eric's desktop, and everyone sat on the

floor with a full plate. "You folks can't imagine how much I appreciate—"

"Got anymore deviled eggs?" Polly's father interrupted.

"Yeah," one of the boys said. "Caleb, pass 'em this way. I want one before they reach Uncle Dan, else I won't get another."

Eric started anew. "Your help has—"

"Someone toss me a roll, will ya?"

"Here you go." Kate pitched it across the room with stunning accuracy.

"I'd like to—"

"Don't suppose you saw any salt in the kitchen, did you, dear?" Paul hitched a shoulder.

Delilah shook her head. "Not a lick." Everyone laughed at her choice of words.

Originally, Eric didn't think Daniel had interrupted him intentionally. With the second interruption, he figured it was simple youthful lack of manners. After the third interruption, he got the message loud and clear. He'd find some way to thank them, though. He opened his mouth.

"So what color did you think about painting the surgery?" Polly gave him an oh-so-innocent look.

"Green." He bit into a carrot. A couple of quick chomps, and he swallowed; then he used the remainder of the carrot like a pointer. "I thought to place my desk back parallel to that wall."

"Do you still want your books upstairs?" Daniel asked.

"Tomorrow I'll purchase a bookcase and fill it. No use hauling the boxes for one night."

"Why don't you use that big old cabinet over there for your books?" Kate tilted her head toward the piece one of the boys was using as a backrest.

"I use that for my medications and instruments. The glass front protects them."

Lunch was over quickly. Polly and her aunt cleaned up as the other girls measured windows and doorways and chattered like a pair of magpies. While the sounds of hammers and saws filled the air, Eric went outside, dipped a brush in wood stain, and started working alongside Daniel.

"Anybody know if the doctor's around?"

"Back here!"

"Get going." Daniel didn't even bother to look up. "Somebody needs you."

Polly appeared in the kitchen doorway. She held a cake of soap and a towel.

"I'm sorry—"

"Your calling comes first." Pouring water into the sink, she added, "I—we understand."

seven

Weary, Eric opened the door to his new place and stopped cold. The smell of fresh paint hit him. For a moment, he had the odd sensation that he'd entered the wrong residence, but the moon cast a weak glow through the window and illuminated his desk.

He blinked in disbelief. He'd forgotten about the Chance men offering to "help out." They'd done far more than just erecting the walls. He stepped inside and lit a lantern.

It didn't take long to walk around the downstairs, but each step brought a small revelation. The walls were complete. Sanded smooth. All of the walls in his examination room had been painted a pale green that looked fresh and calming. Shelves lined one entire wall and the top portion of another.

The old walls in his office were painted: one a buttery yellow, and the other a deeper green. The new walls were stained, and the wood grain gave a dignified feel to the place. Dark green curtains hung in the windows and also across rods in the open doorways. They'd been pulled to the center of the rods and knotted up in order not to brush against the fresh stain and paint.

A glass-fronted, oak bookshelf he'd seen at the store now rested against a wall and contained his precious texts. They'd even been arranged almost in the exact order he would have put them. Polly must've done that. A pair of benches rested against a wall, and brass hooks gleamed in wait for patients' coats and hats.

The place looked. . .professional. It would have taken him weeks to accomplish this. Thanks to the industrious Chances, he'd be able to concentrate fully on his chosen profession right away.

Though the smell of paint still permeated the room, the note he'd seen on the counter reminded him he hadn't eaten in hours. Eric took the plate from the icebox and peeked at what lay beneath the napkin—a mammoth roast beef sandwich and a mound of potato salad. He opened the drawer where he'd plopped his silverware and discovered that a dish towel now lined the bottom and bore a few strategic folds that kept the knives, forks, and spoons separate. After snagging a fork and bumping the drawer shut with his hip, he sat at his desk to eat the supper.

A note rested beneath a jar of flowers. *No pumps at the store. Glad to put one in when it arrives.* Eric leaned back and let that thought settle in his mind. Running water. He'd have the ability to wash things down quite easily and control contagion. Others thought of water as being life-giving because it quenched thirst; to Eric, boiled water meant lives would be saved because it prevented infection.

" 'My God will supply all your needs. . .' " He quoted the scripture softly. *Thank You, Lord, for supplying all of this.*

His grandparents had given him a beautiful leather treatment register when he'd begun to see patients. Not only did he keep a separate file on each family, but the treatment register allowed him a quick overview of the practice and finances. Skipping a page between his eastern clients and the new ones here in Reliable township made sense. Eric opened the register, took another bite, and wrote on the blank intersecting page, "RELIABLE, 1889."

Dipping his pen into the inkwell again, Eric planned what

he'd chart about his first case here. Suddenly, the wonderful taste of roast beef turned to sawdust in his mouth.

Facts. A patient chart contained the specific facts and no emotion. Just the patient information, diagnosis, treatment, and prognosis—but the cold, hard truths in last night's and tonight's cases knotted Eric's guts. A physician wasn't supposed to be emotionally involved. But how could a Christian man—any man—close his heart and soul to such travesty?

He'd just spent hours treating a drunken father and son who shot at one another during an argument. The father didn't survive; the son now lay bandaged on a cot over at the sheriff's. When he sobered up, he'd have to grapple with what he'd done.

Boiling his medical care down to a few brief, stark sentences, Eric penned the information, then waited for the ink to dry. His desk had a deep drawer in which he locked his patients' records. Though everyone would be aware of tonight's murder, last night's travesty at the saloon was recorded in the same book. Eric carefully turned the brass key in the lock.

Mounting the stairs, Eric noticed the rich glow and satiny feel of the just beeswaxed handrail. The room to his left had been painted the same buttery color as downstairs and filled with miscellaneous boxes and crates. As the lamp cast its light in his own room, Eric inhaled deeply.

Deep green paint coated the walls, and insubstantial pale curtains fluttered by the open windows. His wardrobe, washstand, and bed each rested against different walls—all familiar items that made this feel like home. He'd tossed open the trunk lid downstairs to yank out a clean shirt to wear on his call. That trunk now lay at the foot of his bed.

Though the turned-down bed looked inviting, Eric suffered a restless spirit. He took the lantern into the treatment room and lit a second lamp, then opened a box. Unpacking and setting everything in order might help.

≥

"You have a shipment, Polly," Mrs. White called as the bell at the mercantile door dinged.

"Wonderful!"

Eric turned at the sound of Polly Chance's cheery voice. Every time he saw her, the woman had that same bright-eyed, everybody's-best-friend look. The corners of her mouth tilted up naturally, but her lips stayed together. In the last few weeks, he'd seen her weigh her words before she spoke and hold confidences—both admirable traits. If only she weren't so. . .misguided.

"Mama made you some of her blueberry jam, Mrs. White." Polly drew a jar from the basket she carried, set it on the counter, then added another. "And I brought you some tea. I reckoned you'd be running low on it."

Watching them, Eric presumed Polly was bartering. He'd seen the same thing done by every ranch woman in town.

Mrs. White picked up the first jar and held it close to her bosom. "Oh, isn't that just like Lovejoy. You Chances just spoil me."

"We love you. Will you be coming to the bee this week?"

"I don't know. . . ." Mrs. White looked around the mercantile, and her voice trembled. "Without Mr. White. . ."

"We have that covered. You get your choice of a Chance and a MacPherson. Just tell me which ones, and they'll come mind the place so you can get away."

Mrs. White sighed and wiped the edge of her eyes with the corner of her apron, making Eric wonder how long she'd been a widow. Though he'd planned to buy a stamp and send away for more medications to round out his pharmacy, he turned away and secretly pulled the list from the envelope. It might cost a bit more, but he decided to help out the widow by placing the order through her store.

"As I said, you and your mother have a shipment. It's from Salt Lick Holler."

"It must be from Hattie. My brothers have a box out in the wagon to ship to her."

Mrs. White laughed. "I can't figure out how that happens. There's no rhyme or reason to when you trade herbs, but whenever one sends a box, the other does, too!"

"It makes perfect sense. You see, Widow Hendricks taught both Mama Lovejoy and Hattie Thales, so they both follow the same seasonal calendar and phases of the moon."

Eric crouched down to examine a tin of honey just to hide his reaction. The sheer ignorance of what this girl believed was enough to choke him.

"So did you want to order another instrument from the Claflin Company back East with the funds in your account, or did you need something else?"

Claflin? Eric nearly dropped the honey. This woman mail-ordered equipment from the premier medical company?

"I believe I'll wait on that. What I need is some cheesecloth so I can make more tea balls and infusions—and six yards of the bandaging cotton."

The bell over the door dinged again. A young man stuck his head into the shop. Unless Eric missed his guess, this was fifteen-year-old Calvin. Then again, all of the Chance boys looked alike. "Polly, get bullets."

"Okay. Do you need anything else, Cal?"

"Nope." He ducked back out.

Eric felt a flare of satisfaction. He'd recognized the boy, after all.

"Pardon him for being so unsociable," Polly said. "He's not been his best for the last few days."

Mrs. White nodded. "Ulysses MacPherson mentioned he'd tangled with a porcupine."

"I just can't tell you how much we appreciate the way you keep the bandaging cloth wrapped up to keep it clean."

Eric's brows rose. Polly Chance just changed the subject without confirming or denying anything about her cousin's injury. She'd done it so tactfully, Mrs. White probably hadn't even noticed it.

"Six yards." Mrs. White scurried off to the back room.

Eric took the honey to the counter along with a cake of Pears' Shaving Soap. When Mrs. White reappeared, he smiled. "I'd like some of that, too, please. Eight yards."

"Very well." She took off the muslin outer wrap and started to measure. "One, two, three, four. . ." She stopped. "Oh, dear. Six for Polly and eight for the doctor—I don't believe I have fourteen yards here."

Eric waited for Polly to demure. Surely she'd allow that a physician ought to have first call on all medical goods.

She didn't. Instead, she rested her basket on the counter. "How much do you have, Mrs. White?"

Mrs. White continued to measure it out. "Seven yards, give or take a few inches. I'll order more right away. It'll be here in just two days. Polly did ask first. . . ."

"Why don't we share it?" Polly suggested. "Three and a half yards apiece."

Eric had already solved the issue mathematically: If Polly offered to take three yards and he took four, they'd each have half of what they requested. But that was inconsequential. A half yard wouldn't make any difference. Then again, neither would three. "Just sell it all to Miss Chance. I'll have you order me a full bolt so we don't run into this difficulty again."

Mrs. White gaped at him, then stammered, "The factory usually sends thirty-yard half-bolts. Do you want sixty yards?"

He shrugged. "Go ahead and order a half-bolt for me and another for the store. I don't like to be without."

"Those special plasters you ordered came in." Mrs. White gave him a conciliatory smile. "Maybe they'll fill in, in the meantime."

"Good, good."

"Plasters?" Polly asked.

"Oh, they're astonishing," Mrs. White declared. "Dr. Walcott sent off for them—they're the latest thing."

Polly's head tilted to the right. The action made the feather in her hat sway slightly. Under other circumstances, it would be a very charming sight. "What kind of plasters, Doctor? Onion? Mustard?"

"No." He watched Mrs. White fold the cotton. "A company back East makes individual bandages and wraps them separately. They contain healthful powders. I'm able to use them both wet and dry."

"Imagine!" Polly beamed at him. "Would you show me one?"

Eric knew he'd run into these touchy situations. This woman wasn't a peer, and if he treated her as one, he'd implicitly be endorsing her practice. On the other hand, if he failed to use these moments to open her eyes to modern medicine, he could scarcely blame her for her backward ways. If she used old techniques to treat someone when he might have educated her to practice something medically sound, ethically Eric bore the responsibility for that patient's lack of recovery.

Lord, what would You have me do?

eight

"Of course the doctor will show you." Mrs. White lifted a box from behind the counter with a little flourish.

"Johnson & Johnson," Polly read on one of the wrappers. "How very clever of them to come up with such a product! It would be a waste just to open one for the sake of idle curiosity."

Eric swooped in on the opportunity. "Let's put it on your cousin's leg." He snatched the box, took her by the arm, and escorted her out the door. "Where did he go?"

"He's supposed to buy chicken feed." Of all things, Polly laughed. "I hope for his sake, he remembered to buy it in the yellow-and-blue-striped sacks. Aunt Daisy has plans for them."

"So you have chickens? I haven't seen any of the Chances bring eggs to town."

"No small wonder. There are the ten adults, four girls, and fourteen boys, plus a few hands on the ranch!"

"I didn't realize there were that many of you."

"Might be because the church is holding Sunday school for the children. Between my aunts and uncles playing the piano, teaching Sunday school, and ushering, we don't all sit or stay together. Are you from a large family?"

"No." He helped her cross the street. "I'm an only child."

"How sad!" She stopped. "Don't your parents miss you terribly?"

"My mother died in childbirth when I was five. My father sent me back East to my grandparents."

"How dreadful for you and for him." She blinked. "Where is your father now?"

"He's no longer living." Her stricken expression made him soften his voice. "Don't pity me. My grandparents were exceptional people."

"But you have no one now!"

"Which is why I was able to come back to California—I had no one to tie me down." He supported her elbow as she stepped up onto the boardwalk. Now that they were out of earshot, he asked, "Have you had any more headaches?"

"No. I get one or two a month." She blushed but still looked him in the eye. "It was nice of you to check in on me."

"Not that I was able to do much. Feverfew's the best treatment." From his examination, he'd detected nothing abnormal— no evidence of disease or tumors—but other than feverfew and tincture of time, no remedy existed. "I've written back to Boston to see if a neurologist there has any suggestions."

"Mama always said two heads are better than one." Polly wrinkled her nose. "But there are days when one's more than enough for me."

"I imagine so." The stage pulled up, and several folks spilled from it. Discretion demanded he change the topic. He spotted a youngster carrying a huge feed sack on each shoulder. Just the top of his deep brown hair showed. "Is that your cousin coming toward us?"

She stood on tiptoe and craned her neck to see past other folks. "Yes, and he bought the right feed sacks!"

Concerned that if they didn't snag Calvin on his way down the street now, he'd refuse to come into the clinic, Eric said, "Have him set down the bags here at the door. No one will bother them."

"Oh, he'll just dump them into the buckboard." Polly smiled

at him. "Something you'll learn about the Chances—once they set their mind or hands to something, they don't stop."

I was afraid of that. Eric didn't voice his opinion. Instead, he reached out as Calvin drew near. "Here. I'll get this one."

"I'm managing just fine, Doc."

Polly raised both hands in a what-did-I-say gesture. "I warned you that we're a stubborn lot."

Realizing he might have given offense by making it seem as if Calvin couldn't handle the heavy load, Eric chuckled. "At least your cousin has a strong back to match his strong mind."

Calvin shot him a cocky grin, then turned to Polly. "Did you get everything at the mercantile?"

"Not exactly," she confessed. "After you drop off the chicken feed, come here; then I'll finish up."

Her cousin jolted. "Is something wrong? You ailing? Want me to fetch your ma?"

"No, no. Doc has some new plastering bandages."

"From the looks of things when we put up those walls, he's got half the world in there."

"These just arrived," Eric declared. "They're the latest in fine medicine."

Calvin glowered at Polly. "If you lollygag, we'll miss out on April's berry strudel."

"I promise you won't go hungry. I'll make you something—"

"Oh, no!" Calvin backed up.

Color flooded Polly's face. "Hey, my cooking isn't that bad."

"No, it's worse." Cal turned to Eric. "Doc, take my word for it—when the church does box socials or there's a gathering, be sure to avoid Polly's stuff. Otherwise, you'll gnaw your way through half of that pharmacy of yours before you're not breathing fire."

"There's nothing wrong with spicy food. I enjoy it."

Calvin shook his head. "You've got my warning. The woman's a risk to public health."

Eric chuckled. "Why don't you go unload those sacks and come back? After we're done here, you'll be my guests for lunch at the diner."

"Nope." Calvin shook his head.

Eric's heart skipped a beat. He hadn't realized how much he wanted to show Polly the new bandaging plaster. "Why not?"

"Because you keep glancing down. My boots aren't all that interesting, so I'm assuming something"—he glowered at Polly—"got said about my mishap."

"I did overhear something, but Polly didn't breathe a word." His sense of fairness had him vouching for her—the whole situation was taking more twists than a tornado.

"Well, Polly—what do you think?"

"I think even with your strong back, the chicken feed has to be getting heavy. Go dump it and come back. You'll be doing me a favor since I want to see this new plaster."

"Oh, all right." His brow puckered. "But if Doc treats my leg, then we'll treat him to lunch."

Polly nodded. "It's only right." As soon as her cousin clomped off the boardwalk and across the street, Polly gave Eric a rueful smile. "Honesty demands I confess Calvin wasn't wrong. I'm an abysmal cook."

"Then how do you make your curatives?"

A purely feminine shrug lifted her shoulders. "I can follow formulas but not a recipe. It's rather embarrassing, but with seven other women on the ranch, it hasn't been a problem. So I take it you're capable in the kitchen?"

"Not in the least." He couldn't help chuckling. He'd thought that a fault in her—but she'd just held up a mirror and shown his hypocrisy.

"I'd like to pretend it's a trade-off, but Mama's a wonderful cook." Polly smiled at him. "Enough of our shortcomings. I want to thank you for being mindful of Calvin's pride. He's taken quite a ribbing the last few days."

"Family, I've noticed, is allowed to tease. Outsiders aren't."

"That's honest as a robin on a springtime windowsill." She saw his puzzled reaction. "Mama Lovejoy married Daddy when I was five. She's been wonderful to me. I've learned healing, cooking, sewing, and even some colorful 'hill' phrases from her."

"The MacPhersons are from. . ."

She nodded. "Hill country. Temperance MacPherson— Tempy, for short, is Lovejoy's youngest sister. Eunice and Lois are sisters, though I'm sure you noticed the resemblance already. Lovejoy brought the three of them out as mail-order brides."

"I see."

"In all, when both families get together, we make a swarm of locusts look downright pitiful."

"Locusts?" Cal approached. "I'm hungry as a swarm of 'em. How long is it gonna take to make a fuss over nothing?"

"Not long." Eric clapped his hand around Calvin's shoulder and led him inside. "I've never seen a porcupine. Did you save any of the quills? I'd like to examine one under my microscope."

"You've got a microscope?" Polly's voice held nothing short of awe.

"The microscope assists me in making definitive diagnoses in several cases." The doctor headed into his examination room.

Polly stayed at the doorway.

Doc turned and gave her a quizzical look. "Is there a problem?"

"I'll wait out here until Cal's on the table with a blanket over him." Why did heat rush to her face? Oh, she'd done that the first few times she helped Mama treat patients, but that embarrassment was long past. With a few simple measures, modesty could be preserved in nearly every case—and in the few where men needed more frank assistance, Mama cured them. Polly tried to cover for her discomfiture by walking toward the other side of the partitioning wall. "Shout when you're ready."

"Let's get this over with," Cal called out a minute later.

Polly entered the room and went straight for the washbowl. The smell of lye soap filled the air and lent a much-needed sense of familiarity to these impressive surroundings. She looked about. Jars with fancy Latin names lined a whole bank of shelves. On another wall, he'd added glass-fronted doors to the shelves her family had erected. Medical instruments, bandaging supplies, towels, and blankets filled it. "My, you've set up a wondrous surgery here!"

"Thank you." Doc scanned the room. "Your father, uncles, brothers, and cousins couldn't have done a more remarkable job of putting up shelves—and in functional places."

"They were all cousins. I don't have any brothers."

"If the both of you are done gawking at this place and discussing the family tree," her cousin said in a wry tone, "maybe you can see to my leg so I can finally fill my belly."

Polly started unwinding the bandage she'd applied to her cousin's leg early that morning.

"So tell me what treatment you've given," the doctor commanded.

"Porcupine quills have odd little backward barbs that make them hard to get out," Polly began.

"You're telling me," Cal muttered.

"I mixed a cup of vinegar and two teaspoons of baking soda together, then soaked the needles."

"The vinegar burned like anything," Cal tacked on.

"After applying a few doses, it softens the quills," Polly said as if her cousin hadn't complained. "Using hemostats, you grab as close to the skin as you can and pull them out."

"You have hemostats," the doctor said in an even tone.

Polly nodded. "They grab better than tweezers. Quills are anywhere from half an inch to four inches, so you have to be careful not to miss some of the shorter ones." She unwound the last bit of the bandage, baring Cal's leg.

"She got twenty-nine outta me. Stupid critter made me a pincushion."

"After I got them out, I used stinging nettle juice and lemon balm on him to stop the swelling and itch. On the spots that are looking red now, I'm using arnica."

"Arnica," the doctor repeated. He stepped closer and examined the puncture marks. "Why are they all just on this one leg?"

"I stepped over a log. Dumb thing was on the other side."

"I see." The doctor continued to examine the punctures. "That could happen to anyone. I presume your boots protected you to some degree."

"Too bad that stupid critter got away. I would have skinned it and made me new boots from its hide."

"They aren't thick enough or big enough," Polly said.

"Yeah, but Obie and Hezzy said he would have made a fair stew."

"They're welcome to it," the doctor said under his breath. He glanced at Polly and winked. When he straightened, he became businesslike. "Let me apply that plaster now."

From what Polly could see, Doc wasn't afraid of pitching

in and getting his hands dirty. He'd jumped in and pulled his weight on construction day. Judging from the fact that he'd been willing to carry feed sacks, she figured he didn't shy away from carrying heavy loads, either. Then again, she ought to have gathered that just from the fact that his muscular frame proved he was in excellent physical condition. His hands bore no calluses, but the tan line at his wrist told her he conscientiously wore work gloves. It was prudent—a healer had to guard the sensitivity of his or her fingertips.

His hands were wonderful—long fingered, large, and strong, yet he possessed remarkable deftness. Polly watched as he demonstrated step-by-step with exacting moves and words. He would have made a good teacher, and his competence was undeniable. Afterward, he looked at her. "Do you have any questions?"

"Yeah," Cal said. "Can you stop talking so I can pull on my britches and let us go eat? No use in the two of you trying to heal me at the same time you let me starve to death."

The doctor led Polly into the other room. He sat at his desk, and she sat on one of the new benches. "Once you remove that plaster in two days, I recommend using the arnica," the doctor said.

Polly nodded. "That Johnson company is very clever to have invented those."

"Yes. Medicine has come a long way. There are many inventions and discoveries." Eric ran his knuckles across the smooth surface of his desk in a long, slow arc. "Old ways are phasing out as we learn improved methods of treatment and care."

"I'm ready." The green curtains parted, and her cousin came in. "Bet we're not home five minutes before you have Aunt Lovejoy gawking at this newfangled bandaging."

"There are always new things to learn." Polly cast a smile at the doctor. She had the feeling she'd learn a lot from him.

≈

Later that week, furious pounding and a holler, "Doc!" made Eric race for the door. He needn't have bothered. John Dorsey threw open the door, nearly tearing it off the hinges. "My wife's in labor!"

Delighted to be called out for a maternity case, Eric quickly grabbed his bag. "Congratulations. How far apart are the contractions?"

"I don't know."

Since so many folks didn't own timepieces, that answer didn't surprise Eric. He simply closed the door, mounted his gelding, and asked, "Are they far apart or close together?"

"Couldn't rightly say."

"Then did her water break?"

"How would I know?" John rode out of town at a demented pace.

After riding up abreast of the man, Eric said, "Last I saw Beulah, she looked full term."

"I hope to shout. The carryin's been hard on her."

Now that he'd managed to get John to calm down a bit, Eric went back to gathering information. "So how long was her last labor?"

"Don't know."

Eric couldn't recall ever having a less informative father-to-be. "How many children has she had?"

"This'll be her fourth in six years." John sat a bit straighter in the saddle. "My first."

That explained a lot. "Congratulations. Tell me, when did her pains start?"

"Honest, Doc—I don't know!" John shot him an irritated

look. "Can't talk sense into her. She and her mother took the little ones off to a quilting bee over at Chance Ranch. Tanner rode over to tell me I'm due to be a papa."

"So where is Beulah now?"

"At the bee."

nine

Visions of rust, rye whiskey, and an ax loomed in Eric's mind. He nudged his mount to go faster. When they reached Chance Ranch, thirty or so children were racing around, climbing trees, and playing on rope swings. If that wasn't enough activity, most of the Chance men were fitting logs together in order to expand one of the stables. At the edge of that utter pandemonium, a dozen and a half women sat around a pair of quilting frames.

"Beulah!" John roared. "What're you doin' sittin' there?"

"I'm stitching," she answered back. "What're you doing here?"

"I fetched Doc. You're supposed to be havin' our baby."

"I am." She poked her needle into the quilt, curled her hands in a white-knuckled grip around the frame, and moaned.

Polly sat on one side of her. She set to rubbing the small of Beulah's back. Lovejoy wafted a silk fan toward Beulah.

Eric dismounted and headed toward them. "How far apart are the contractions?"

"Middlin' close," Eunice MacPherson volunteered.

Eric couldn't imagine what business she had, sitting out here with her new babe. She ought to still be lying in her childbed. He chalked that up as yet another example of poor judgment on the part of these self-proclaimed midwives.

Looking over his shoulder, Eric addressed John: "How long will it take for us to transport her back to your place?"

"The only place I'm going," Beulah said, "is inside. You don't mind, do you, Lovejoy?"

"Not a lick." Lovejoy stood, as did Polly. Polly dragged Beulah's chair back.

"I was hoping to finish this quilt afore I birthed this babe," Beulah said in a mournful tone. "With four little ones, I'm not going to have time to do much quilting for a while."

"We'll finish it for you," several of the women said.

John tried to pick up his wife to carry her inside.

Polly stopped him. "Your wife needs to walk. It's good for her."

"How long was your last labor, and how long have you been contracting?" Eric nudged his way between Lovejoy and Beulah.

The laboring woman took two more steps, then stopped. "Three hours." She started to moan again.

John braced her arm; Polly stepped in front of the woman and started swaying her as if they were going to waltz. He didn't criticize her. These little things—odd as they were—could be ignored. He'd save his objections for things that really mattered. No doubt existed in his mind that several important issues would come up during this delivery. Then, too, he'd have more success in having Polly see the errors of her ways if he spoke with her privately instead of in front of half the women in Reliable.

Polly's eyes met his. "In case you're not sure which question Beulah answered, it was both. The last labor lasted three hours, and she's been at this for just about three hours."

When the pain eased, Beulah let go of her death grip on Polly and started to shuffle ahead. "I don't have a gown or blanket here for my baby."

"You know how our Laurel loves to sew," Lovejoy said. "I got me a whole stack of baby clothes jest in case, and Alisa crochets more baby shawls than I can keep count of."

Eric made a mental note of that fact. He had all of the medical supplies, but he assumed mothers kept the essentials on hand. In a situation like this, he supposed he'd have wrapped a baby in that soft white bandaging cotton, but women cared about minor details like that. He'd ask Mrs. White to order a few infant blankets and gowns for him to use in emergency situations.

"I don't think I can do this," Beulah whimpered.

"You're doing beautifully," Polly praised as she continued to assist the laboring woman toward the cabin. "We'll help you."

John walked backward in front of his wife. "I got Doc for you. He'll know what to do."

I certainly do, and I'll be sure to deliver this child with the best of medical technique.

Beulah stopped again. Eric thought it was for a pain, but Beulah straightened up. "I want Lovejoy and Polly."

"But—"

Lovejoy let out a crack of a laugh. "Ain't nobody pushing t'other away. Doc and us—we'll all work together."

"I want my mama, too."

Eric knew better than to argue with a laboring woman— especially one asking for her mother. "Of course your mother is welcome."

"And—" Beulah's eyes opened wide, then narrowed into a squint as she began to let out a guttural moan of a woman bearing down.

Polly jerked Beulah's face toward hers. "Blow. Blow. Come on. Blow."

Deciding this had gone on far too long, Eric swept Beulah up and strode into the cabin. Someone had already folded back the blankets and covered the bed with oilcloth. Left to their own timetable, these women would have Beulah standing in a barnyard, dropping the newborn on his head in the dirt as chickens pecked the ground around him.

As he laid Beulah down, Polly quickly robbed the woman of her shoes and stockings. John called from the doorway, "You take good care of my wife!"

Beulah's mother hobbled up and shoved the toddler she was carrying into John's hands. "You see to this one for a while." She shut the door in his face. "Doc, you turn away. It's not fittin' for you to stand there whilst we peel off her gown."

Eric couldn't care less about those issues at the moment. He needed to set out his equipment and scrub. A towel covered a small table by the bed. He swept it off, only to reveal an array of hemostats, scissors, and gauze—all things he'd have chosen for the case.

"They've all been sterilized in boilin' water," Lovejoy said from over at the washbasin. "C'mon o'er here and scrub up."

Beulah's mother smoothed a sheet over her as Polly hung the dress up on a peg. From the sound of logs thumping loudly into place and hammering, the men weren't in the least bit concerned about the goings-on. Eric had to admit to himself that so far, their confidence appeared to be well placed. These women seemed to have everything under control.

Then Polly went to a door and opened it.

Narrow shelves lined the wall of the dank room she'd revealed. Bottles, jars, and jugs filled them, and bunches of leaves hung from the ceiling. Until now, he hadn't realized the full extent of the "medical practice" these "healers" exercised. It was a marvel they hadn't killed off all of Reliable with their quackery.

Grim determination swept over him. He had to protect this mother and baby. "Shut that door!"

❧

Polly looked at the cabin door, thinking John might have burst in to check on his wife, but it was closed. She gave the doctor a startled look.

"I said, shut that door." Using swipes as harsh as his voice, he dried his hands and headed toward Beulah.

"I need to get the rust—"

"I have ergot in my bag."

Mama shrugged. "I'm shore it'll work jest fine. Beulah, we need to—"

"Mrs. Dorsey," Doc said as he shoved a hand beneath the sheet. "I'm going to examine you."

Polly dug through the doctor's bag and found a vial of ergot. "How much do you want me to measure out?"

"Zero point two milligrams. It will be exactly one level scoop of the smallest spoon in the adjoining pocket."

"Okay." Polly efficiently measured out the drug and said nothing about how abrupt Doc had become. Maybe it was his way of handling the awkwardness of such an intimate situation. Maybe he felt a tad nervous. She tossed out the used water, refilled the pitcher with freshly boiled water, and began to scrub.

"Breech," Doc announced.

"Last two were, too." Mama patted Beulah's arm. "You done fine with them. Wanna do the same as we did t'other times?"

Beulah nodded.

Doc straightened up. "We're not doing anything. The precept with breech deliveries is to allow the child to descend on its own."

"Hands off a breech," Polly recited Mama's ironclad rule.

"Exactly."

Beulah didn't care about their conversation. She'd started bearing down again. When the contraction ended, her mother bathed her face with a cool rag and murmured encouragement.

Polly stepped up beside the doctor. "Ready?"

Mama nodded, and Beulah weakly said, "Yes." They turned

her onto her side, then helped her up on her knees. As she gripped the headboard, she moaned. "Jesus better give me a boy. John's wanting his firstborn to be a son."

"Son or daughter, he'll love 'em," Mama reassured.

Doc glowered at Polly and yanked her aside. "What are you doing?"

"Kneeling widens her hips. Beulah has big babies."

"We'll discuss this later." He headed back toward the bed.

Things happened fast after that. Just another two pushes, and the baby spilled out onto the bed. Mama dried it off, and Doc made sure it could breathe. They each grabbed a hemostat to clamp the cord, but Doc cut it. While Doc handed the baby to Beulah's mother, Polly helped Mama lie Beulah back down.

Doc's jaw dropped in astonishment when he pivoted toward the bed. He didn't say a word. Polly supposed since he wasn't accustomed to a woman kneeling, he hadn't taken the next logical step of realizing the simplest thing to do would be to lay the woman down so her feet were at the headboard.

Twenty minutes later, Polly stood at the footboard next to Doc and grinned at Beulah. They'd gotten her all cleaned up and turned around, and Doc had given her his special ergot powder. Since Doc was present, they'd covered Beulah with a shawl when the babe started suckling.

"I heard a cry—what's going on in there?" John Dorsey shouted.

A chorus of giggles from the quilters filled the air. "Thirty minutes," several of them called out.

"Thirty minutes?" Doc gave Polly a wary look.

"It's the rule. A new daddy tends to get underfoot, so Mama makes them all wait half an hour to come in."

Mama nodded. " 'Tis reasonable. Lets a babe eat well and

a mama have a chance to remember 'twas love, not pain, that brung the child."

Doc shoved the vial into his medical bag and latched it shut. Ten minutes later, satisfied Beulah and the babe looked fine, he opened the door. "Congratulations, John. You have a healthy son."

John plowed into the cabin. Doc grabbed Polly by the wrist and yanked her out the door. The man made a charging bull seem tame.

Kate, April, and Laurel all popped up from the quilting frame and dashed toward Polly in a flurry of calico and petticoats. The last thing she needed was them to get an earful of the doctor's opinion. She felt certain whatever he had to say, it wasn't going to be mild or kind. Emphatically waving them off, Polly stumbled alongside the fuming man.

He towed her around the cabin, away from everyone. Finally, he stopped and faced her. "This can't go on."

ten

"What are you talking about?" Polly gave him an exasperated look.

"That!" The doctor waved his arm toward Mama and Daddy's cabin. "It was unbelievable."

"I thought it was beautiful."

Air gusted from his lungs in a loud huff. "You had no business being there. You're untrained and unmarried."

Quite literally, Polly dug her heels into the earth. She planted her hands on her hips and leaned forward as she hissed, "I've assisted with over four dozen deliveries and performed eleven on my own." Straightening, she tacked on, "As for unmarried—you are unmarried, too!"

He scowled at her. "We are not discussing my status. I'm a licensed physician. You, on the other hand, think a handful of flowers and a headful of wild notions are all it takes to effect a cure."

Never once had anyone faulted her for following her calling. Patients were thankful, and her family did all they could to help her. Thoroughly shocked by his accusation, Polly stared at him. Behind her, her friends chattered at the quilt and her cousins constructed their building. They were all building things up; all Doc wanted to do was tear down.

He shook his head. "I'm sure you mean well, but medicine is a science."

"Healing is an art. It's a gift from God."

His jaw hardened. "I agree it is a gift, but God expects us to develop our talents so we use them wisely and well."

"Let me get this straight." Polly stared at him. "You've decided you're the only person qualified to help the sick and injured of Reliable."

He gave her a curt nod. "You're able to treat minor injuries, but—"

"And you're turning up your nose at flowers and such because you send away to a pharmacy back East for fancy prescriptions."

"Patients deserve the best we can give them."

"Oh, I see. According to that logic, the herbs God made aren't as good as something a pharmacist sticks in a bottle."

"Now wait a minute—"

"No, you wait. We were happy when you answered the ad to come to Reliable. Mama ran herself half-ragged until I grew old enough to assist her. Between the two of us, we've stayed more than busy, caring for our neighbors and kin. Some things, we couldn't treat—and we knew it full well. We've sent folks to San Francisco for surgery."

"That won't be necessary anymore."

"I know. That was one of the reasons I was glad you responded. Mama's not saying much, but I can see how her back's bothering her. I've tried to take over more, but I can't handle everything on my own, either."

"That won't be necessary anymore."

"You're welcome to think whatever you want, but believing something doesn't make it true. You yourself said earlier that God expects His children to use their talents wisely. I'm not boasting when I say I'm called to heal. It's not me—it's God working through me. His herbs, flowers, and roots bring relief to folks. Just because you suddenly come here and decide you're the only king of the hill doesn't mean everyone else has to get off the mountain!"

"There's a right way and a wrong way to do things—"

"Those are the first words you've said I can agree with," she interrupted hotly. "And you messed up horribly back there. What gave you the right to announce Beulah's news to everyone?"

Doc Walcott gave her an icy stare.

"Everyone knows it's the new mother's joy to tell her husband what God gave them. You went and spoiled her fun after all her pain." Polly shook her head. "Back East, they might do things differently, but that doesn't make it any better or any more right. You're here now."

"And I aim to stay and do my best for everyone."

"Well, I aim to stay and do my best, too."

❧

"The road to hell is paved with good intentions," Eric muttered to himself as he rode back to town. He already knew that adage. Well, today proved it—and he'd seen firsthand that weeds-, leaves-, and berries-lined road. Those Chance women merrily dished out whatever concoctions suited their fancies as treatments for the supposed diagnoses they made.

And how did they make reasonable, rational diagnoses? They had no microscope. They had no medical training. Granted, he'd seen Polly employ some of the more standard treatments such as camphor, but that didn't endorse her skill. It merely proved the law of averages that occasionally she accidentally stumbled across a correct remedy. All he had to do was remember Lovejoy rubbing Perry's open wound with a plant she called "toothache" to remind himself that, left to their own devices, Polly and her mother could very well kill or maim patients with the simplest of maladies.

Truly, he wondered how so many women had survived their birthing techniques. Rust and rye whiskey. Kneeling on a bed and lying upside down on it. Putting an ax under the bed to cut the pain! Mothers announcing the gender of the baby—it was utter nonsense in the least. At worst, it was life-threatening.

Not only had he seen Lovejoy rub a flower over an open wound, but Polly had volunteered how she'd applied vinegar and baking soda to porcupine needles. The former was unsanitary; the latter made no sense whatsoever. Vinegar was acidic; baking soda was alkaline. By mixing the two, she'd canceled out the effectiveness of either. On a scientific level, the women defied every rule. Only by the compassion and mercy of God had this community survived.

He'd held his opinion for long enough. Instead of barreling into town and declaring himself the only one able to help the ill, he'd given Polly a chance to prove herself. In his practice back East, he'd met a few women who quietly, efficiently worked alongside physicians and gave excellent, practical bedside care. Never once before coming here had he imagined he would have to wade through rivers of nonsense—however well-intentioned the women might be.

Eric didn't regret for one minute the fact that he'd finally taken a stance. He didn't even regret the fact that he had pulled Polly aside and put her on notice. After all, the Good Book taught that when a Christian had a problem with another, he should take that person aside and try to reason with him or her in private.

But she'd looked so. . .shocked, then angry. He'd have never guessed beneath her calm facade, Polly could turn into such a virago. *Then again, I could have chosen my words more carefully. I didn't use much tact.*

Fretting over what he'd set in motion wouldn't accomplish anything. Eric tried to formulate a plan of attack. First, he'd continue to practice superlative medicine so his patients and their families would understand the level of his knowledge and ability. Second, he'd behave civilly toward Polly—but he'd not mentor her as he'd originally planned. Third, he'd need to think of another woman who might be a good surgical assistant and nurse for him on the occasions when he required an associate. Finally—and most importantly—he'd go to the pastor.

Yes. He liked Pastor Abe. The man exerted a calming influence on his flock. Seeking wise counsel and having the minister mediate with the Chances would be biblical. It would also remain confidential. That way, Polly and her mother wouldn't be open to public censure.

Satisfied with his plan, Eric reached town. He hitched his gelding to the rail and went into his office. Once there, he opened his patient register and smiled as he wrote, "Delivered Beulah Dorsey of her fourth living child. Breech. Male, seven and one-half pounds. Mother and child fine."

He locked away the book, then noted a small piece of paper on the far bench. Eric strode across the floor and picked up the scrap. It had been folded several times. As he opened it, several black needles rolled into his hand. Loopy letters in pencil formed uneven lines across the paper: *You said you wanted to see porkypine needles. Plaster itched. Took it off. Cal*

Eric sat on the bench and let his head thump against the wall. The Chance clan was a good bunch. Salt of the earth. They'd welcomed him and fixed up his place, and he'd even discovered they and the MacPhersons donated the land, lumber, and labor for the church. How could they have reared Polly to be such a good-hearted, wrongheaded, strong-willed woman?

The grating sound of boots on the boardwalk made Eric shoot to his feet. It wasn't seemly for him to be loafing about.

He had no more than tucked the porcupine needles back into the paper when an older woman rapped on the screen. "Dr. Walcott?"

"Come on in."

"I just wanted to get a recommendation for a cough elixir."

"Please come in, Mrs. . ." His brows rose in invitation.

"Greene. Violet Greene." She gave him a weak smile.

"Please, have a seat. Tell me how long you've had the cough."

"Oh, no." She let out a trill of laughter. "I'm in the pink. It's my grandchildren. Davy's children. They're fine all day long, but come nightfall, they'll be croupy again. Mrs. White at the mercantile said you might have a suggestion."

Mrs. White. God bless her soul, she's been a voice of reason since the day I arrived. "There are a few elixirs I recommend or blend, but it depends on the patient. I'd have to examine the children when they're in distress."

"Sounds sensible to me." Mrs. Greene pleated the material beneath her fingers in an unconscious show of nerves.

"Do the children worsen at night, then improve during the day?"

"Yes. That's exactly it! My Davy never did that, but all three of their children do. It's positively nerve-racking."

"Would you like me to come by after dark to see it firsthand?"

"Yes. Oh, please. That would be wonderful. Thank you for offering. We live in that cottage back behind the smithy."

Eric gave her a reassuring smile. "Fine. Come nightfall, I'll drop in. We'll see if we can't get everyone squared away."

Mrs. Greene scurried away, and Eric stayed busy for the afternoon. He enjoyed a plate of pot roast for supper at the diner, dallied over a fine slice of apple pie, then returned to his office. He read up on children's respiratory ailments before packing additional medicaments specific to croup in his bag and walking down the street. By the time he drew abreast of the smithy, seal-like barking filled the air.

Eric knocked on the cottage door, and the moment David Greene opened it, the smell of eucalyptus and berries assailed him. A woman in a huge cape stood by the stove with a baby on her hip. She spooned something into his mouth. Eric didn't need her to turn around. He knew just from the unique tone of her murmur that Polly Chance was interfering with his patients.

eleven

"Doctor?"

Polly tensed at the sound of Davy Greene's one-word greeting. *What is the doctor doing here?*

"Oh, it's the doctor." Violet Greene let out a nervous laugh. "I asked him to come see the children."

"Well, I asked Polly to come while I was at the quilting bee," Davy's wife said in a sharp tone.

Polly intentionally kept her silence. Everyone in Reliable knew Davy's mother and his wife didn't get along. Violet hadn't exactly approved of Marie as a prospective daughter-in-law, and when Marie suddenly inherited a niece and nephew, Violet announced the engagement was off. Davy and Marie went behind her back and visited the pastor. Since then, strife had filled the household.

Davy shuffled into the room, took stock of the situation, and did his best to make peace. "With four youngsters, it doesn't seem unreasonable for us to have Polly and Doc both here."

Polly set down the spoon and used her right hand to unfasten the ties of her cape. That action would let the doctor know she had no intention of leaving. Hanging it on a hook on the brass hall tree, she stated, "I've already dosed this one with my elixir."

"Then you go ahead and see to him; I'll treat the other three." Doc set his bag on the table and reached for the closest child.

Teddy scooted between the chairs, ducked under the table,

and raced over to cling to Polly's skirt. Just that exertion set him wheezing.

Polly stooped down and wrapped her arm around him. "Remember my rule? When you sound like your daddy's accordion, no running."

"Here, Doc." Violet shoved the little four-year-old toward Dr. Walcott. "This is Madeline. Maddy, Doc'll fix you up."

"Hello, Madeline."

Madeline tilted her head back and measured how tall he was, then burst into noisy tears. The baby in Marie's arms started crying, too.

"Look what you've done. It's worse now," Marie snapped at her mother-in-law.

"I was just trying to help!"

"Let's all settle down." Doc scooped the baby from his mother. "I need it quiet in here so I can determine where the constriction is."

"It's never quiet around here," Davy muttered.

Teddy's blue-tinged lips sent Polly into motion. "Violet, you hold Eddy. I need to get some medicine into Teddy."

"What are you giving him?" the doctor demanded.

Polly resisted the temptation to simply state, "An elixir." Instead, she listed the contents of the herbal combination. It was the first medicine Mama Lovejoy ever gave her, and just the scent of it brought back memories. If Doc dared to say one bad thing about it, he'd regret it.

He gave her a stern look. "I prefer to treat this with camphor inhalation."

"Camphor's what I use on the baby, too. The older ones have runny noses and watery eyes, so they need more than just that." She waved toward her satchel on the table. "I've got a tin of camphorated salve in there."

"I brought some, thank you."

So much for trying to cooperate. Polly spooned elixir into Teddy and put him on the settee. Maddy clung to her like a limpet.

"My turn."

"Go ahead." Doc's begrudging tone made it clear he was making the best of a bad situation. His look told her she was the bad situation.

Whatever he thought, however he acted—that wasn't important. The patient always came first. Polly clung to that precept and concentrated on the children. She gave Marie a reassuring smile. "Dressing the children in these flannel vests was a good idea."

"I sewed them for the children," Violet boasted.

Polly nodded sagely as she rubbed her hand up and down Maddy's back to calm her cry so she'd be able to swallow the medication. "I'm low on red flannel, Violet. Do you have any left over?"

"I'll go check." Violet bustled out of the room.

Doc opened his bag and took out a hornlike wooden stethoscope. Pressing it to the baby's back, he closed his eyes and listened.

He closes his eyes—just as I do. The realization irritated Polly. Why did something that minor make a difference? But it did. She'd discovered shutting her eyes helped her concentrate more fully on the sounds.

Polly turned away and picked up a clean spoon. She set Maddy on the table, measured out the elixir, and coaxed the little girl to take it.

Sticking two fingers in the air, Maddy bargained, "Two spoons and no stinky."

Polly tucked Maddy's braids behind her. "One spoon of the

medicine is just right for a girl your size."

Maddy's wheeze accelerated. "No stinky!"

They'd been through this on other occasions. Maddy hated the onion and mustard poultices. Polly didn't fault her for it—though effective, they reeked. She'd anticipated this. "I brought something special, Maddy. Could you please open my satchel?"

With tears in her eyes and her lower lip protruding, Maddy fumbled with the clasp. When she opened it, Polly urged, "Look inside."

Maddy's eyes grew huge. She yanked out the surprise. "Dolly!"

"A special dolly." Polly had asked Laurel to embroider a face and hair on pink flannel. It buttoned onto a triangular red flannel "dress" with little hands and feet sticking off it. "This silly dolly likes to eat smelly onions and mustard! We're going to fill her tummy with them, then you get to hug her close."

While Maddy played with the doll, and Teddy and Eddy held mice Polly had made from a handkerchief, she chopped onions and started butter melting to make poultices. In no time at all, she wrapped the poultices in Violet's red flannel. After having done this so many times, she automatically made a fourth one.

Doc swiped the teakettle from the stove and thumped it down on the corner of the table. It made considerable racket, and he mumbled an apology. Camphor fumes radiated from the baby in his other arm. "Mrs. Greene, why don't you sit beneath a steam tent here with the baby?"

When both of the Mrs. Greenes moved toward him, Polly grabbed Violet. "Could you please refill the reservoir on the stove and fill a pot to boil? We'll need to steam all the children."

Polly caught the silvery glint in Dr. Walcott's gray eyes and didn't know how to read it. Was he angry she interfered, or was he glad she'd just averted another squabble? The hot poultices wouldn't allow her time to ruminate over that. She handed one to Davy. "If you'll pop this under Teddy's vest, I'll get Eddy."

"I'll examine Eddy first." Doc's declaration came in a rare silence among all the children's coughs.

Unwilling to argue, Polly simply grabbed a poultice and wiggled her forefinger to beckon Maddy.

"Is that for my dolly?"

"Sure is. See how it makes her tummy all happy and full?" Polly stuffed the poultice inside. "You need to cuddle the dolly and make her feel at home."

The doll worked. Maddy gleefully allowed the reeking poultice to rest against her chest. She wrapped her arms around it. "Rocky-bye, baby," she crooned to the doll.

"Yes, that would be wonderful. You go ahead and sit in the rocking chair. I'll cover you and the dolly with your favorite blanket."

Doc opened his jar of camphorated salve. Polly cleared her throat. "Teddy can inhale that, but he breaks out in a rash if you put it on him."

"Now there's a fact," Davy agreed. "Gets the same rash from playing with cats, too."

Doc capped his jar. "Croupy children are more prone to such sensitivities. We'll steam treat him. The eucalyptus I'm smelling in here ought to serve."

The children all started to breathe better. The harsh coughs softened and lessened. Marie reappeared from beneath the towel with the baby fast asleep. Polly took the two unused poultices and put them in the warming section of the stove. Marie winked at her, signaling she'd seen where they were and would use them if necessary.

Polly took the poultice out of the dolly and let Maddy continue to hold it while Teddy and Eddy still clung to their little hanky mice. Mama Lovejoy had done that, too—given Polly and her little sister something soft to hold and love when they were sick and scared. From the day Polly had received her own healing satchel, she'd made it a habit to include handkerchiefs or bandanas so she could create instant "loveys" for her young patients.

"Davy, if you warm their bed, we'll bathe them—"

"You're not tubbing croupy children!" Doc glowered at Polly.

"The water's warm," Polly reasoned. "The room's warm. The bed will be warm. They won't chill, and it gets the fragrance off of them. Besides, a little extra steam would probably be a good idea."

"I'm all stinky." Maddy wrinkled her nose.

Doc leaned down and cajoled, "You don't want your dolly to catch a chill, do you?"

"The water's not cold." Maddy gave him an angelic smile. "Dolly won't get her hair wet."

Doc threw back his head and laughed. He tugged on one of Maddy's braids. "You're a charming little minx." He looked to Marie. "If you heat the towels in the oven so we keep the children warm afterward, I'll approve of a quick steam bath."

Polly drew a little flowered dimity "sack" from her satchel. "This is your dolly's dress for when she feels all better. Mama or Grandma will wash the other one."

"How clever!" Marie happily unbuttoned the red poultice.

"Good thing," Violet muttered. "I didn't want that thing reeking up my bed."

"I thought that Maddy and the boys all slept together." Polly frowned.

"It's too crowded." Marie lifted her chin. "But someone"—she cast a dark look at her mother-in-law—"keeps tucking them back in the same bed."

"When did you start this new arrangement?" Doc strode toward the small, rumpled bed in the corner.

"A week or so ago." Davy's voice held a weariness that made it clear he'd been stuck in the middle of another ongoing battle.

Doc pushed aside the quilt and sheet, then shoved one pillow toward the foot of the bed. As he reached for the next one, Polly groaned. "Don't tell me that's a down pillow."

"It is." Doc held it up and scowled.

"Polly told us not to have feather pillows." Marie gave her mother-in-law a look that would scald water.

"I concur." Facing Violet, Doc dropped the pillow and folded his arms in an unmistakably stubborn stance. "You asked me to come treat the children. I will not be responsible for patients when they or their families fail to follow explicit instructions. This was dangerous. It's no wonder the children are in distress."

Violet burst into tears, snatched the pillow, and stuffed it in the fireplace. "I never meant to hurt them. I love my grandbabies. Truly, I do!"

" 'Course you love us," Maddy said as she wound her arms around Violet's legs. She stood on tiptoe and whispered loudly, "Don't be mad at me, Gramma. I'll sleep with you now."

"Madeline Marie Dorsey." Davy's voice took on an ominous tone. "Have you been—"

"She just missed Teddy and Eddy." Violet petted Maddy's hair. "When she's a little older, she'll want to sleep in my big bed."

Marie collapsed into the rocking chair. "You mean—"

"I think the children will be fine once you square them away in bed," Doc cut in. He looked at Polly. "Surely you won't be going back to the ranch tonight."

Normally, she spent the night here in the rocking chair, minding the children when they took ill. She clasped her satchel shut. "Actually, Mrs. White's been terribly lonely. I think I'll keep her company tonight."

After saying their good-byes, Doc swept Polly out of there fast as could be. As they walked toward the mercantile, he cleared his throat. "I've found children who rash and wheeze are more sensitive to apprehensions and nervousness within the home."

Polly didn't abide gossip, but she conversed with Mama about cases. It made sense she and Doc would also discuss situations. She chose her words carefully. "Perhaps this will be an opportunity for them to. . .um. . .clear the air. It would be nice for everyone to breathe a little easier."

He nodded. "Thanks for warning me about applying camphor on that little boy."

Polly stopped. "You and I might not see eye to eye, but I promise you, I always put my patients first."

Doc studied her in silence. He gave no reply and started walking again. Silence hovered between them as he saw her to Mrs. White's. Polly thanked him for walking her in the dark, then slipped inside.

"My, my. The doctor taking you on a walk," Mrs. White cooed once the door shut.

Polly gave her a stern look. "We were treating patients. There was nothing in the least bit personal about him seeing me safely to your door."

"Oh. Well." Mrs. White's starry eyes made it clear she didn't believe Polly for one second. She headed upstairs. "Come on. I'll brew a pot of tea. Could you please close the windows? It's getting nippy."

Polly made it upstairs and put down her satchel. Drawing back the edge of a drapery so she could reach the window more easily, she spied the doctor down the street. He was talking to one of the soiled doves on the corner by the Nugget.

twelve

House call on David Greene family. Baby's distress from croup alleviated with camphorated rub and steam tent. Other three children suffering from respiratory affliction. Eddy inhaled camphor; reportedly allergic to contact of same. Teddy and Maddy treated by lay healer with elixir of unsubstantiated contents, mustard and onion poultices, and steam bath. Feather pillow and family strain exacerbating the children's health.

Eric waited for the ink to dry, then turned to the next page and dipped his pen in the inkwell. *Kitty recovering from her ordeal. Still anemic. Recommended she ingest liver thrice weekly and take to sipping beef broth.*

Again, he allowed time for the ink to dry, then locked up his book. Hungry, he headed toward his kitchen shelves. Underwood's deviled ham spread on a handful of Dr. Graham's crackers would provide him with a pleasant snack as he studied the porcupine needles under his microscope.

Indeed, his shelves boasted the finest in healthy fare. An abysmal cook, he normally depended on the local diner. Physicians didn't have the luxury of living by a clock, though. That being the case, Eric made it a habit to keep modern, convenient foodstuffs in his kitchen. Quaker Oats, Joseph Campbell's beefsteak tomato in a can, Libby's Vegetables. . .yes, he'd managed to make do on many occasions.

The next morning, he set oats boiling. Eric rather liked his morning schedule—he'd awaken, use water from the reservoir to start breakfast, then do calisthenics. He'd wash and shave, then dish up the oatmeal. Allowing the oatmeal to cool slightly, he'd finish dressing. A bowl of oatmeal, a piece of fruit, then quiet time with the Lord. By seven fifteen, he'd take a morning constitutional, then return and see patients.

Today he'd taken his bag along on his walk with the intent of checking in on the Greene children. Polly was slipping out of the cottage as he arrived. He inclined his head. "Miss Chance."

"Good morning, Doctor." Her smile could have coaxed out the sun. "The children are ever so much better."

"Wonderful." He still planned to check in on them himself.

She stepped to the side, pulled a knife from a leather sheath at her waist, and proceeded to neatly slice several leaves from a plant. The scent of mint filled the air.

"What are those for?"

Tucking the leaves into the pocket of her apron, she shrugged.

"You just chop up leaves for the sake of it?"

She concentrated on fastidiously wiping her knife on a strip of cotton cloth she'd produced from a different pocket. "I didn't chop them up. I merely harvested them."

"Why?"

"Because." She slid the knife back into the sheath and looked at him. "It's wise to take advantage of the supplies God sets before us."

"And what will you use that for—or should I ask whom?"

"I can't say."

"Can't," he gritted, "or won't?"

Polly's face puckered in frustration. "Both. I don't discuss the persons or maladies I treat because patients deserve privacy."

"Under other circumstances, that would be admirable, but I've already pointed out this cannot continue. Interactions are known to occur between different medications. If you give someone an herbal remedy before or after I prescribe something, it could be disastrous."

"Then you have two choices: you can either ask the patient, or you can tell me whom you treat and why."

"We both know I'd not break my patients' confidentiality." He glowered at her.

"Then you'll simply have to make it a point to question your patients about what remedies they've attempted before seeing you." She gave him an innocent smile. "I always do. It's astonishing what they'll try before seeking competent assistance." With that galling comment, she pivoted and let herself back into the cottage. "David, the doctor's come."

Well, at least she hadn't left him standing out there. Eric stepped up to the threshold. "Good morning. I came to see how the children are."

"Everyone's just fine," David said.

Eric would have been delighted with that news if it hadn't been for Polly and Violet standing over by the stove, whispering as Marie lifted the lid of a teapot that let out an unmistakably herbal aroma.

૨૨

"Nothing," Mama Lovejoy said as she lifted her face to the sky, "showers a body with joy better than the rays of the sun."

Polly laughed. "Mama, you said that selfsame thing about last week's rain."

"I reckon I might have, but that's no matter. Joy's a fleeting thing—you gotta snatch it up with both hands every chance you get."

They dismounted and put their gathering bags on one of the picnic tables out in the yard. Mama said she'd spotted flowering currant over on the border of the Dorseys' when she'd gone to pay a visit to Beulah. Though Mama still liked to walk and gather each morning, Polly suggested they ride over and collect some of the shallow roots in order to preserve the integrity of the plants they had in their own patch. If they cut into their patch, the supply wouldn't flourish or be available in an emergency.

"Need some help?" Kate and April traipsed over. Kate pulled string from her pocket. "I figured you'd want to hang leaves to dry."

"Surely do." Mama started separating things from her bag— roots at one end of the table, leaves toward Kate, and strig heavy with black currants in the middle.

"Oh, black currants!" April perked up. "You know how I love black currant jam!"

Polly and Mama exchanged a fleeting glance. They'd actually collected the fruit in order to extract the juice to use as a diuretic. Then again, they'd decided to go gather more in a day or two. By boiling down the juice, a special sugar called rob could be extracted—and nothing worked better on sore throats. Polly winked at Mama.

"April," Mama said as she held up some of the currants, "my mouth starts to waterin' jest at the thought of the jelly you and yore mama're gonna make of these."

"I'll go get a bowl."

Laurel joined them. "For being so pretty, why do those have to smell so awful?" She handled the currants by the strigs and avoided the leaves.

"You like horses and cattle, and they smell pretty bad, too," April teased as she set a huge red glass bowl on the table.

"I keep my distance from the cattle and ride in a buggy or buckboard whenever I can," Laurel answered with a giggle.

"Dear Lord above made us all different," Mama said. "Yet look how we live in harmony."

"I don't know about that harmony, Aunt Lovejoy." April leaned forward. "I heard Dad tell Uncle Daniel that Pastor asked them to bring you and Polly in for a meeting tomorrow. Tanner thinks the doc's behind it."

"No reason for ever'body to get het up." Continuing to sort through her gathering bag, Mama didn't even trouble to look up. "We all want what's best. Sometimes, folks jest need to have a meetin' of the minds."

Mama's wise words usually gave Polly a sense of serenity, but this was different. Doc didn't think she or Mama had any ability. In fact, he'd intimated they posed a danger to those they treated. Folks in Reliable township and the outlying area had depended on the Chances for medical care for sixteen years—but would they suddenly side with Doc, now that he had arrived with an office full of fancy stuff and a medical degree hanging on his wall?

Laurel, Kate, and April all wanted to be wives and mothers. Polly—well, she wanted those things, too, but being a healer was her calling. She'd never once imagined anyone would try to take that from her. The community had grown enormously. It stood to reason that there were more than enough folks needing help that the doc wouldn't be able to handle them all on his own.

"Mercy me, how many currants did you pick?" April asked as Mama headed toward her horse. She raced over and helped untie Mama's other bag from the saddle horn. "I've got it for you. You're better at tying leaves. Go ahead whilst I sort through this."

Polly flashed April a look of thanks.

"You gals are such a blessing." Mama stretched gingerly. "If it grows much hotter, them currants might droop. Cain't take the sun, you know. Mayhap we oughta think on goin' back today—"

"What a good idea." Polly nudged Kate's foot. "Kate and I can go do that while you remove Perry's stitches. Uncle Bryce and Tanner could come along and scout around for the hive."

"Hive?" Laurel shivered. "I'll stay here and help with the jam."

❧

By midday, Polly plopped down on a log next to Uncle Bryce and surveyed the full buckets with a sense of satisfaction. "When we get home, we'll start pressing the juice right away."

Tanner chuckled. "May as well. You're already stained clear up to your elbows."

"You have no room to speak," Kate countered.

"Yeah, well, Uncle Bryce set me to digging up those roots, so you can complain to him."

Bryce shook his finger at Tanner. "Lovejoy taught me to make a paste from them to cure cattle. You'll be glad we have it one of these days."

"We ought to make you scrub the dirt and honey out of your shirt." Kate eyed their shirts with obvious dismay. "I don't think it'll come clean in a month of Sundays."

"You'll scrub however long it takes so I'll give you some of the beeswax for candles," Tanner shot back.

"Brothers are an affliction." Kate sighed. She gave Polly a resigned look. "Do you have a cure for that?"

Polly looked at the siblings and smiled. "Mama says love and time cure a lot."

Uncle Bryce brought the lunch bucket from the buckboard. He pulled an apple from it and handed it to Polly. "Here's the cure you need most."

"Oh?" She accepted it.

"An apple a day keeps the doctor away," he recited in a voice that held a slight edge.

thirteen

"Then she can have mine," April said, offering her apple.

"You're only saying that because you want my share of the cheese." Polly tried her best to change the topic. The whole thing had snarled into a huge mess. April was still interested in the doctor. Polly realized she was, too—but that only made this whole betrayal worse. He'd turned out to be arrogant and condescending.

Times like this, she almost let down her guard—but Mama drilled into her the necessity of minding her tongue. Things were already brewing—the last thing she needed to do was turn up the heat. "Nobody makes better cheese than Aunt Tempy, and I aim to eat my fill."

Tanner scowled. "I used my knife to get those roots for you. Is it okay to use it on the cheese?"

"The roots are for the cattle, not for me to use as curatives." Polly grabbed for the bucket. "Even so, I don't think there's a problem, because if I don't miss my guess, Laurel and Aunt Delilah already cut the cheese into wedges. We won't have to slice it at all."

The cheese tasted great. The apple—well, the first bite reminded Polly of Tanner's words. An apple a day. . .yes, she'd like to keep the doctor away. She took a second, savage bite and chomped on it. By the fourth crunch, though, the flavor turned. Polly took yet another taste, then rotated the apple and spied a bruise on it. Without hesitation, she pitched the fruit as far as she could.

That night, back in her cabin, she snuggled under the quilts and tried to go to sleep. She'd been fighting a sick headache all evening. Laurel squirmed closer and half-whispered, "Are you going to be okay tomorrow?"

Polly moaned. She hadn't realized Laurel suspected she had a headache.

Laurel poked her. "Need me to come along?"

"What good would you do?" April asked.

Laurel sat up. "I'd sit beside her and glower at the doctor while I prayed."

Polly groaned—more from the loud pronouncement than the fact that Laurel stole all of the blankets when she sat up.

"I'll go, too," Kate promised loyally. "We all promised to stick together, and this is one of those times when unity counts most."

"That's right." April sat up and immediately unraveled her night braid. Within seconds, it was undone and she'd started to wrap her tresses with rags.

Oh, this is a mess. Laurel's ability to glower is nonexistent. April will bat her lashes and flirt, and Kate can't sit still, so she'll squirm the whole time. I've got to put an end to this right away. Trying to ignore the pounding in her head, Polly said, "Hold on a moment. I appreciate your support—"

"No need to thank us, Polly. You'd do the same if any of us was in a fix." Kate sat up and swiped the rags from April. "We're going to back you up, so we'll be somber as judges."

"And we'll wear our black dresses," Laurel tacked on.

"We're not mourning!" April cried.

"We're protecting our Polly." Laurel dragged Polly upright and wrapped her in a surprisingly fierce embrace. "How dare that man call her before the pastor as if she were morally flawed."

Morally flawed? Polly spluttered at that assessment. "Now just—I—"

"Don't you worry, Polly." Kate wrestled the hair rags from April again. "We'll vouch for your character."

"I'm not worried. Well, at least, not about my character," Polly amended honestly as she managed to peel herself from Laurel's clinging embrace.

"But you are worried, and we'll be there. I'll talk to Eric—"

"April," Polly said in her firmest voice, "You will not—"

"Call the doctor by his first name. It's simply far too forward," Laurel cut in. "You'll be silent. We all will. Uncle Daniel and Uncle Gideon will do the speaking, and when it comes up, I'll be the spokeswoman for our cabin since I'm the eldest of us."

"Polly's older," April muttered.

"You can't expect her to stand there and proclaim her innocence," Laurel pointed out.

Polly couldn't believe the speed at which her cousins chattered. This conversation was moving faster than a locomotive in full steam. "Everyone quiet down and listen to me."

The girls all hushed.

"I appreciate your support, but you're not going. Mama is attending the meeting with me, and it's best to keep matters like this discreet."

"Discretion is important," Laurel said slowly. "But then maybe just I ought to go along."

"Not fair!" April protested.

"We are more like sisters than cousins, and we're sisters in Christ." Polly took a deep breath. "But there are times each of us is going to need some privacy."

"Privacy, around this ranch?" Kate snorted.

"I've been accustomed to having a measure of solitude,"

Polly said slowly. "Don't get me wrong—I love you all being here with me now. It's just that with my healing, I still have times when I must handle confidential matters. I've resolved that tomorrow will be such a time."

"You can't go alone," Laurel gasped.

"Daddy, Mama, and Uncle Gideon are accompanying me. I don't want the doctor to feel as if the whole Chance family is ganging up on him. As much as I appreciate your caring sentiments, you're all staying home." Polly looked around the loft and met her cousins' gazes. "That's the way it's going to be."

Laurel pursed her lips for a moment, then nodded. "Then we'll fast for breakfast and lunch and support you in prayer."

"We don't have to fast to pray," April objected.

"And it's our turn to cook tomorrow," Kate pointed out.

"The Bible says, 'Where two or three are gathered...,'" Laurel began.

"Well, we're four here. We'll storm heaven's gate with prayers." Kate bounded out of her bed.

Polly gave in to the need to bury her head in her hands as the headache exploded.

"Don't despair, honey." Laurel stroked her arm. "God will help you."

"I have faith, but I'm also fighting a headache," Polly whispered tightly.

"Then you just lie back down. Kate, get her a cool compress. I'll get the feverfew. April, you track down where the oil of peppermint is that the doctor used. We'll take care of Polly and pray downstairs all night long on her behalf."

"No sleep?" Kate moaned.

"It's better than fasting," April said.

Polly scrunched down in the bed and pulled the blankets

over her head. She couldn't even handle her cousins. How would she ever deal with the doctor tomorrow?

&

When Eric heard the Chances arrive, he stepped back deep into the parlor. He'd intentionally arrived a little early. Since he'd requested this meeting, it was only fitting that he be here first. Through the window, he could see they'd come not on horses or in a buckboard, but in a buggy he'd not seen before.

"Hello, Mrs. Abrams." Polly gave the pastor's wife a hug.

"Hey there," Mama said as she smiled and gave Mrs. Abram's tummy a loving pat. "Ain't you jest fat and sassy-lookin' today?"

Joyous laughter trilled out of the pregnant woman. "Isn't it wonderful? God has blessed us, indeed."

Pastor Abe shook hands with Gideon and Daniel Chance, then motioned toward the parlor. "Come on in."

Eric remained standing and solemnly shook hands with the men. Though this would be awkward, he'd found that civility often mediated in such situations. It didn't escape his notice that Daniel Chance had his arm about his wife's waist and Gideon kept a proprietary hand on Polly's arm. These men were protective, and one look made it clear they didn't appreciate being brought before the minister. *The matter is even touchier than I thought it would be.*

"Why don't we all sit down." The pastor's words rang out as a command, not a suggestion. Good. He didn't kowtow to the Chances simply because they were major benefactors of the church.

"Lovejoy, you sit in the rocker. It's easiest on your back," Mrs. Abrams trilled.

Daniel seated his wife and remained standing by her. Eric sensed the man would turn to stone ere he ever left her side in this situation. Thankfully, the pastor shoved a chair behind the stubborn-looking man, and Daniel grudgingly forced himself to sit down. Gideon steered Polly to the settee and sat beside her. He slid his left arm across the back of the settee and curled it around Polly's shoulders in a move that nearly shouted, *Watch yourself, mister. This is my niece you're calling on the carpet.*

Lovejoy's face looked open and guileless as it always did; Polly's features looked strained and pale.

Maybe she's coming to realize things have to change.

"It's so nice to have you all come pay us a visit." The pastor's wife perched on the piano stool. "Would you all care for some lemonade, tea, or coffee? I have strawberry pie, if that influences your decision."

The pastor cleared his throat. "Sweetheart, this isn't a social visit."

She popped up. "Oh, dear. I'm so sorry."

"Oh, you go ahead and sit yoreself back down—but someplace more comfortable," Lovejoy said. "Ain't nothin' being said that needs to be kept secret, and I cain't abide the thought of pushing a woman outta her own parlor."

Eric would have preferred the matter to be handled without an audience. Then again, after this got settled, someone would need to subtly spread the word that he'd be handling all of the community's medical needs. He eased into the one empty chair—an ornate rosewood piece built low to the ground and suited to a woman. His knees folded up ridiculously, so he eased them out until the toes of his just-polished shoes missed the hem of Polly's gown by a mere inch.

It didn't escape his notice that Polly kept her face averted.

"I'd like to start with a word of prayer," Pastor said. "Heavenly Father, Thou art all-wise and all-knowing. We implore Thee,

Handful of Flowers 115

be among us and grant us wisdom and grace. In Jesus' precious name. Amen."

Well, that was a fine prayer. A great opening to this. With God going before me, surely the road will be smoother and straighter.

"Doc Walcott came to me with some concerns," the pastor started in. "Apparently he's discussed the issue with Polly already, but they didn't reach a satisfactory agreement."

"He's spoken with you, Polly?" Her father's tone carried astonishment.

She nodded but gave no details.

"Actually, we've spoken twice." Eric cleared his throat. "The matter is rather delicate—"

"What?" Daniel Chance bolted to his feet. His hands knotted into fists, but to his credit, they stayed at his sides. "My daughter is not that kind of woman. There's no way she'd be—"

"Oh, dear me," Mrs. Abrams said, her voice fluttering.

"No. No!" Eric held up his hand. "You mistake my meaning."

Daniel glowered at him. "Choose your words better. I'll not have you slur my daughter's reputation."

"Dan'l, he misspoke. Ain't a one of us who hasn't done the same." Lovejoy slipped her hand into her husband's. "Jest go on ahead and speak your piece, Doc." Humor glinted in her eyes. " 'Tis plain you got our attention."

"Thank you." He nodded his head in gratitude and respect. He'd not spent much time with Lovejoy, but she exuded warmth and kindness. If anything, that made him feel worse about the whole matter. "What I meant to say is that the topic I'm broaching is sticky."

"Get on with it," Gideon said. He took up more than his half of the settee, and he'd wrapped his arm more tightly around his niece.

"In the past, Mrs. and Miss Chance have done their best to

care for the people of Reliable."

"And they've done a wonderful job of it, too!" Mrs. Abrams chirped.

Eric wouldn't stand for many more interruptions. He forged on ahead as if nothing had been said. "But now that I've come, they can relinquish their responsibilities in that arena."

There. He'd said it diplomatically, but the issue was out in the open now.

"Me and Polly're happy as a sparrow with two worms that you come to our town, Doc." Lovejoy tugged on her husband's hand. "I told Dan'l it'll be a blessing to have someone hereabouts to handle surgery and such."

"He wants us to stop everything, Mama." Polly's words hung in the air.

Gideon and Daniel exchanged a grim look. The pastor's wife burst out, "But you promised you'd deliver my baby!"

"Yes, well—" Eric began.

"And we will." Polly's voice held quiet resolve.

"I mean no disrespect, Doctor, but I can't imagine. . ." Mrs. Abrams blushed to the roots of her hair. "Well, I just. . .you know. Besides, this baby wouldn't have ever come into being if it weren't for Polly and her mama."

Eric folded his arms across his chest. "That baby, Mrs. Abrams, came into being because God willed it and due to the—"

"Watch it," Gideon cut in.

Eric stared at the head of the Chance clan. "You've just underscored part of the problem. Lovejoy and Polly are ladies. There is no denying that medical practice necessitates dealing with intimate and personal issues."

"Precisely." The pastor's wife finally relaxed. "I'm so glad you understand, Doctor. I just couldn't ever have a man attend me when my time comes."

"I assure you, Mrs. Abrams, I've delivered many children. Maintaining modesty is quite simple by the application of a few draping sheets. Medical training prepares a physician to attend a woman with the latest in scientific advances."

"Far as I know, babies have always come the same way," Polly said tightly.

"Now let's jest calm down. Doc, Polly and me, we're happy to serve folks however best we cain. There's more than enough to keep us all busier than a fly at a hop-toad party. Nothin's a-wrong with us partnerin' up."

Everyone else in the room—the pastor included—smiled as if the matter had been settled amicably. Eric heaved a sigh. They simply didn't understand. He was going to have to be blunt. "There may be sufficient work, but knowledge is lacking."

"We'll teach you what you need to know about folks. I recollect from when I moved here how it takes time to figger out the peculiarities. Folks all have some odd little kinks and pet remedies or notions you have to work 'round."

"Mama, that's not what he's saying."

Eric looked at Polly. She remained tucked into her uncle's side and couldn't even bear to face the room. . .or him. He'd known she enjoyed dabbling with her herbs, but the depth of her sadness cut at him.

But I have to do the right thing.

"A handful of flowers and a few medical instruments amount to medieval medicine." Eric looked at Daniel. "In the past, you didn't have anything more than that. I don't doubt that your wife and daughter did the best they could with what they had. It's just that the time has come for change. Medical science has made astonishing discoveries and advances. We've abandoned treatments that were once standard and turned to superior methods in their place."

"Seems to me, folks can decide who they want to give them care," Daniel said in an all too reasonable tone. His hand slid over Lovejoy's in a move that said he'd far rather entrust his life to her care than any doctor's.

"They can't make wise decisions when they still think the world is flat, because Polly and Lovejoy navigate by the same principles that were used centuries ago!"

"The world is round, Doc. Ain't nobody gonna fall off." Lovejoy gave him an earnest look. "But you got my solemn promise that iff'n I got me a patient who's close to the edge, I'll send 'em yore way."

She tried to rise, but her husband had to assist her. Pain flickered across her face, and Eric wanted to offer his help—but knew it would be ill-advised at the moment. Lovejoy gave him a long look. "Now that we've got things settled, I'm taking my girl home."

Polly rose, but she didn't do so with her usual grace. The way she'd spoken so little and used muted tones suddenly took on a completely different significance. When she instinctively averted her face from a stream of sunlight, Eric gritted his teeth and demanded of Daniel in a low tone, "Why did you bring your daughter if she's fighting a migraine?"

"The family respected her choice. Fools that we were, we hoped this meeting would resolve the strain so she could rest."

Gideon's brow furrowed. "Polly, go on out with your mama. We'll be on momentarily."

Lovejoy reached up and pulled Polly's head onto her shoulder. Polly tenderly wrapped her arm about her mother's waist and stroked a few times before bracing Lovejoy's back. Slowly, silently, they shuffled from the room. The sight of them wrenched Eric's heart—mother and daughter both in pain, each trying to be mindful of the other's infirmity. More than ever, he wanted to relieve them of trying to care for the people of Reliable. They had their hands full with one another.

Mrs. Abrams toddled out behind mother and daughter, fussing over them.

Once they were out of earshot, Eric appealed to Daniel to be reasonable. "They're struggling."

"They're just having a bad day," the pastor said.

Eric shook his head. "The problem's existed a long time. It's why your township advertised for a physician. I'll relieve them of the burdens of caring for the town. In the end, we all have to admit that it's the best thing for them as well as for the folks of Reliable."

Daniel's feet widened in an aggressive stance. "I give folks the benefit of the doubt. There was a time I wouldn't have, but Lovejoy changed that about me. Right about now, Doc, you're skating on mighty thin ice. We want you here. We need you here. But I won't stand for you insulting my wife and daughter."

"I meant no offense. It is a matter of patients deserving the best of care. I truly regret the fact that such a concern casts a shadow on them. They've given their best; it's just not good enough anymore."

"There's a line between confidence and pride, Doc." Gideon strode toward the door. "You just crossed it."

The Chances all left then, and the pastor walked Eric out to the hitching post. "Thanks for trying, Pastor." Eric swung up into the saddle.

"It'll take awhile, but I believe you'll all iron this out."

Eric looked down and nodded. "In medicine, that's called tincture of time, but I'm not sure that's all it'll take in this situation."

"Have faith. In my profession, I've seen God work miracles."

"Well, Pastor, I'll gladly treat you for free if you develop knee problems from kneeling and seeking heavenly intervention."

fourteen

"Miss Chance."

At the sound of Doc's voice, Polly's three cousins immediately spun in a swirl of their Sunday-best dresses. She hesitated.

"Now I suppose that was predictable." The doctor's tone held wry amusement.

Ashamed of her attitude toward him, Polly turned.

Doc smiled—an easygoing, lopsided grin that made him look downright neighborly. "At least the Chances only had a handful of girls instead of a bumper crop of them like they do boys. If I called Mr. Chance, I'd be mobbed."

"Doctor," April cooed, "the Chances and MacPhersons have given leave for people in Reliable to call us by our Christian names. With such large families, going by our surname becomes confusing."

Polly watched as Kate reached back and pinched April's arm to hush her. Reasoning with April hadn't done any good, because she considered the doctor to be exceedingly handsome and imminently eligible. If she didn't stop acting like a henwit, she'd embarrass herself and the doctor.

"Very well." Dr. Walcott focused in on Polly. "Miss Polly, I'd like a word with you."

"We're in charge of Sunday school today, Doctor."

"All of you? How is it that all the Chance gals are doing the Sunday school together? I thought you usually split up two by two."

"Like the creatures on Noah's ark?" Kate teased.

Doc chortled. Polly wished he hadn't. At the moment, she didn't want to like him, and he was being impossibly charming.

"I've noticed the parishioners all take turns." He drew closer. "Why don't I come along?"

"Do you like children?" If April perked up anymore, she'd be on tiptoe.

"Definitely." Doc deftly stepped to Polly's side. "What is today's lesson for Sunday school?"

"Ephesians 4:32." Polly felt more than a slight twinge when she answered the question. "Be ye kind one to another. . ."

"Tenderhearted," the doctor joined in, "forgiving one another, even as God for Christ's sake hath forgiven you." He spoke the words softly, solemnly. Polly couldn't interpret the look in his eyes.

Soon they sat in a big circle out on the grass. Kate led the singing, and Polly couldn't help enjoying the doctor's bass voice amid the childish sopranos.

April read the Bible verse; then Laurel gave a short lesson.

"Why don't we take time to share how someone was kind to us this week?" Polly's suggestion resulted in a sea of waving hands. "Birdie, hand me Judy, and you share; then you may pick whose turn it is next."

Birdie handed over the soggy toddler, then popped to her feet and yanked a small tin item from around her neck. "Pa bought me a chewin' gum locket at White's."

"And she shart the gum with me. 'Twas hardly e'en chewed yet!"

Birdie scowled at her sister. "I didn't pick you to share next, Vinetta."

"How wonderful that she couldn't wait to tell us all what a grand sister you are," Polly said.

"You are a grand sister, Birdella. Iff'n God let me pick a sister, I'd pick you."

"Now that showed tenderheartedness, just as today's verse said." Doc gave the sisters an approving nod. His quick thinking impressed Polly. He'd managed to praise the children and keep their focus on the lesson.

"Let's have Octavius take a turn," Vinetta suggested, and Birdella nodded.

Doc followed Polly over to a table, where she started to change Judy's diaper. Her cousins hated that task, so she handled it as a matter of course. They'd continue to monitor the children.

Doc leaned against the table and fleetingly touched the puffed sleeve of Judy's little dress. He said quietly, "Is there something special about gold and the MacPhersons? It's the only color I see them in."

Polly smiled. "The MacPhersons hail from Hawks Fall and Salt Lick Holler, where they could barely eke out a living."

"I recall you saying Lovejoy brought the women out for arranged marriages."

Polly nodded. "Uncle Obie wanted his children to know they weren't growing up poor, so he bought a whole bolt of fabric. By using flour and feed sacks for collars, bodices, and pockets, my aunts managed to dress the entire clan, but then they realized they'd have a problem with hand-me-downs if they changed color."

"Why?"

"The younger children would be dressed in golden yellow, and the older ones would be in other colors—so the littler ones would always feel as if they were left out of getting anything new."

"That could pose a problem."

Polly nodded. "Hezzy thinks gold looks fine with Lois and

Eunice's red hair, so the family decided they'd stick with gold. That way, they look like a family, and hand-me-downs aren't apparent. The manager at the feed store is smart enough to always have a selection of yellow-toned bags just for them." She shot Doc an amused look. "I'm so accustomed to the gold, I forgot about it until you just pointed it out!"

"I suppose I have no room to speak." He glanced down at his chest and tacked on, "I always wear white shirts."

Thankful they were keeping the conversation light, Polly smiled. "You mentioned that the day we worked on your office. My cousin Cole said he can't decide whether you're trying to look like a pastor or a penguin."

"To whom does Cole belong?"

"Miriam and Gideon. It's easy to tell by how the children are named."

"Enlighten me."

"The girls are named whatever the mother fancies, but the boys' names are chosen by letter. Miriam and Gideon's sons all have C names."

"Caleb, Calvin, Cole. . ."

"Yes, and Cory and Craig are over by April. She's their sister. Then the boys belonging to Alisa and Titus begin with T: Tobias, Tanner, Terrance, and Troy. Kate is their daughter."

"So that leaves Delilah and Paul with the Ps," he deduced. "I've met Parker and Perry."

"Patrick, Paxton, and Packard are in the sanctuary."

"And. . ." He thought for a moment. "Lauren is their daughter?"

"Laurel." The fact that he hadn't gotten Laurel's name correct surprised Polly. Feminine and soft-spoken, she managed to catch the attention of every other man in the county.

"I suppose the MacPhersons all wearing gold is my only clue

for them. It'll probably take me months to sort out that clan."

"Just listen for names. Tempy and Mike love to read, so their children have Greek or Roman names. Lois and Obie named all their tribe after the disciples—but they made allowances for Johnna, Jamie, and little Judy here."

"Very clever."

Polly then muffled a laugh. "If it's an odd name, you can be certain the child is Eunice and Hezzy's. We do our best to tag a nickname onto each of the children so they won't be teased mercilessly."

"Birdella is Birdie." His brow rose in a silent invitation to provide more.

"Meldona is Melly. Register is Reggie. Benefit is Benny..." His gray eyes reflected growing astonishment as she mentioned each name. She let out a sigh, "No one's come up with anything for poor Lastun."

Doc's eyes twinkled with mirth. "Let me guess. That must have been the one before Elvera."

Polly nodded. "Eunice declared he was the last one she'd have. I guess it's proof God gets the final word on everything."

"Indeed, He does." He swiped Judy from her and obligingly made a funny face when the toddler poked him on the nose.

She washed up at the bucket, then helped Craig with the fastener on his overalls.

"Your father and Lovejoy didn't have children?"

Polly willed him to understand. "She couldn't have any of her own, but Lovejoy's children are all around you. Her hands catch, soothe, and cherish them."

He didn't look away or pretend to misunderstand. Instead, the doctor gently shifted Judy to his other side, cupped her head to his shoulder, and swayed from side to side as if he'd fathered half a dozen children himself. His thumb absently played with a wispy auburn baby curl at Judy's temple. "They're blessed to have the love she gives."

"Then why are you trying to stop her? Why are you trying to stop us?"

The corners of his mouth tightened, but he kept his voice gentle. "Polly, I couldn't ever stop you from loving your family and neighbors. I'm just freeing you from the responsibility for their health so you can help them in a thousand other ways."

Judy stuck her middle and fourth fingers into her mouth and started sucking on them. Her eyes drooped, and Doc cradled her as she fell asleep. He absently rubbed his jaw along her carroty curls, then said, "I heard back from the neurologist. Unfortunately, there's no specific cure yet, but he suggested your headaches might be caused by something you ingest. The list he sent included red wine—"

"I don't partake of alcohol."

"So you've said. But I wondered about oranges. He mentioned with California shipping oranges back East in abundance, he's noticing a connection there."

"No, I love oranges."

"Nuts?"

She shook her head.

"Aged cheese." The doctor looked at her steadily.

Thunderstruck, Polly stared back at him. She enjoyed those other foods without any trouble, but. . . "Tempy's cheese," she said. "I love it. I never connected that, but before the last two—no, three—headaches, I'd eaten a wedge."

"Well, then, let's hope you have far fewer migraines now." Instead of sounding smug as he might have, his tone carried sincerity. He turned when someone called for him. "Yes?"

Perry pointed at his arm. "I told 'em how you came to buy a horse, but you drew a pitcher on my owie 'cuz I got hurt."

A girl giggled. "That's a funny way to heal somebody."

"It worked. I'm all better," Perry insisted.

"And we praise God that you're strong and healthy now." Doc wandered around the edge of the clump of children. "Don't you all think the way God makes us better is proof of His kindness?"

"Maybe forgiveness, too." Perry's face puckered. "I wasn't 'posed to be jumpin' outta the hayloft when I got hurt."

"God doesn't always heal us when we're sick, but He is always faithful to forgive us." Doc continued to hold Judy's sleep-lax little body as he imparted those wise words. "We have to tell Him we're sorry for the wrong things we've done. The Bible verse today talked about being kind, tenderhearted, and forgiving. God is all of those things. Because we are His children, we want to be like Him."

"You're not a children," little Craig hollered.

"Sure I am." Doc stood there, tall as Gulliver in the Land of Lilliput. "God is my Father. No matter how old I get, I'll always be His child."

"Like Mama is all growed up, but she's Grampa's little girl?"

"Exactly."

Polly leaned against the small table and tried to clear her mind. Dr. Walcott confused and confounded her. He loved children, was called to heal, and seemed to be a strong believer—all things they held in common. They weren't trivial things—they were soul-deep values. If it weren't for his absurd notions about who could care for the sick, they'd undoubtedly get along very comfortably. She and her family had done everything they could to welcome him. Why couldn't he get past his selfish pride and accept her help?

April came back toward Polly. From the awkward way she carried Lastun and crinkled her nose, Polly assumed he needed his diaper changed. April laid him on the table and whispered, "Dr. Walcott really does adore kids, doesn't he?"

"Yes."

"He'll make a good father," April said in a dreamy tone.

"You're too young," Polly hissed.

"It's not like you want him for yourself," April snapped back.

Polly didn't respond. Then again, she couldn't. She wasn't sure whether it was the truth or a lie.

fifteen

Eric straightened up from his microscope and reached for the mug. By habit, he raised it toward his mouth, but the pungent smell of vinegar caused him to set it back down. A cup of coffee would taste great, but he wanted to finish this experiment.

Deftly, he removed the porcupine needle from beneath the microscope. Indeed, the end bore nasty little barbs as Polly had told him it did. Each of the ten he'd inspected were the same in that regard—though they varied in thickness and length. He'd mixed vinegar and soda in the exact proportions Polly mentioned, and now he would dip three of the needles in it to see how they reacted. Three, he'd grind up and see if he could determine what minerals they were comprised of. The other four—well, they'd be interesting things to add to his collection of oddities.

Someone knocked on his screen.

"Come in." He stopped dipping the quills and set them aside on the corner of a towel.

One of the workers from the feed store tromped in. "Doc, I'm just fine, other than, well. . ." He shifted from one foot to the other. "My guts are all bound up."

Eric took him into the treatment room, asked several questions, palpated the man's belly, and took down the jar of *cascara sagrada* to measure out a dose. "This ought to do the trick."

"Oh, good." His patient paid a nickel for the exam and

medication, then wandered back out.

As Eric put the jar away, he mentally translated the Latin name. *Cascara sagrada. Sacred bark.* His hand stilled for a moment. Setting the jar farther back on the shelf, he stood eye-level to feverfew. Bark and flowers. Two of the common cures he dispensed were simply dried from nature and pulverized into a fine powder.

But I base my prescriptions on years of training, sound medical examinations, and scientific knowledge. Who knows what possesses Polly to dispense herbs or her mother to employ her odd treatments? Besides, my pharmaceuticals are of standardized strength and produced in a sterile environment.

He went back to his experiment. When he lifted the porcupine quill from the soggy towel's edge, Eric stared in disbelief. The vinegar solution had actually softened it! How had Polly learned such a trick?

And what else does she know? Is it possible I could experiment on some of her herbal compounds and discover if there's any scientific basis to her remedies?

Even Hippocrates advised using willows' yellow leaves or bark to help with aches and pains. From back during the Revolutionary War days, a doctor had distilled digitalis from purple foxglove to help certain heart problems. But Eric's supply of those medicaments was, again, standardized and reliable.

Oil of cloves, magnesia, bromide of potash, boric acid crystals and powder, zinc carbonate, ether, and morphine—his shelves and cabinets contained almost the complete pharmacopoeia. Each compound filling the vials and bottles could be vouched for in purity and efficacy. The memory of that dingy room off Lovejoy's cabin that held the jugs and jars of the Chance women's homemade apothecary renewed his doubts.

To be sure, a fraction of their so-called treatments would probably be effective, but that didn't make those women safe practitioners. Modern medical science demanded proof—experiments that rendered the same results when repeated. Those women practiced by trial and error, by folklore and fanciful thinking.

He eased back. Perhaps he could meet Polly and her mother halfway. He'd inspect their apothecary and approve of certain substances, then convince them to agree to limit their practice to treating cases of croup, mending sprains, and stitching up minor wounds. Surely those maladies comprised a large part of their practice anyway. He'd "review" proper technique with them and update their practices so they'd not indulge in dangerous oddities like rubbing a flower near an open wound.

Then he'd take care of the rest of Reliable's medical needs.

It all seemed so easy. . .but the longer Eric stood there, the less comfortable he felt. Gideon Chance had told him flat out he'd been prideful. Indeed, he had. In fact, he'd hoped Polly would understand when he spent time with her at Sunday school that he was trying to make peace.

It wasn't that he was wrong. It was just that he needed to be sure he framed matters carefully so no one's feeling were hurt and Polly and Lovejoy still felt useful. Confident in his stance, he'd failed to weigh the human factor—a mistake he'd not repeat. Surely if he overtly showed approval of the things the women did well, he could either teach them better methods for what they did wrong or simply convince them to refer such cases to him. Yes, Lovejoy was right—this could become a partnership of sorts.

Partnership means both parties bring something to the table. Polly knows the community well. In fact, Lovejoy offered to guide me past some of the "peculiarities." That would be a terrific help, he mused as he continued to look at his supplies.

Oil of cloves. . .oil of eucalyptus. . .morphine—they were all plant-based. Zinc and magnesia were minerals. For that matter, lye soap came from leaching acid from ashes. Perhaps what he needed to do was view Polly's collection as a source of something that might add to medical science. Much of it might be nonsense, but a few gems might well shine in the darkness of that closet.

Excited by that prospect, Eric grabbed his coat and hat. He'd pay a call on Miss Polly Chance. Maybe they could be partners, after all.

&

"Polly." Uncle Bryce stepped into her cabin and shut the door behind himself. "That doctor is out here. Wants to see you."

"Dr. Walcott?" She gave her uncle a startled look.

"Ain't no other doctor 'roundabout here. I'm sticking to my guns." Uncle Bryce gave her a stern look. "I don't like you keepin' company with him."

"I'm not 'keeping company' with him." Polly set aside the herbs she'd been grinding and stood.

"Hmpf. My brothers all said the same thing 'bout women who showed up here; then they up and married 'em. This guy might be rich and smart and handsome"—he waggled his finger at her—"but you remember what I told you."

Polly patted him on the center of his chest. "You don't need to worry."

"My Daisy's in town, or I'd send her out to keep watch over you. Where are your cousins? Most always, they're a gaggle around you. Now, when you need 'em most, they're nowhere to be seen."

"They're visiting Beulah and the baby, and a good thing, too! If they heard you liken them to geese, they'd be offended."

"Truth is truth." He squinted at her.

"Oh, honestly, Uncle Bryce! I understand why you all send the kids along with Caleb for his courtship with Greta. They're young and foolish. I'm twenty-one, and I'd like to repeat: This is undoubtedly a professional consultation."

Uncle Bryce snorted. "I don't believe that for a second. The man's already said you're dangerous. He couldn't care less what you think about medicine; he cares what you think about him. I'd still feel a heap better if at least one of the girls was here to vex you and that man. That'd make him keep his distance and stop any stupid notions or designs he might be concocting."

Polly decided not to argue the point. Mulishly stubborn, Uncle Bryce wouldn't let go of a notion any sooner than a coyote would yield a meaty bone. She straightened up and waved a hand downward to call his attention to her attire. "Look—I'm not even taking off my work apron to go meet him."

He held her back. "Hang on a minute and tie the belt looser. Cinched in so snug, it makes you look like a girl."

"I am a girl." Laughing, Polly opened the door and walked across the yard. More than a few men in the area knew she was a girl—they'd asked Daddy permission to pay her court—but not a one of them managed to pull it off. Simply put, they were nice—but for some other woman. None of them ever made her heart sing. Then there was the doctor. Polly wondered if he even thought of her as a woman instead of as a pain in the neck.

"Hello, Doctor."

"Miss Polly." Doc doffed his hat. "Since you're interested in botanicals, I thought perhaps we ought to compare notes."

Taken by surprise, she stammered, "What kind of botanicals?"

"Healing ones. Your garden is quite impressive. Perhaps we could start there."

"Oh. Okay." She took a few steps toward the pump and rinsed out a bucket. "If you don't mind, I need to gather a few things."

"I don't mind at all." He sidestepped when Cory, Packard, and Terrance ran past.

Perry skidded to a halt. "Wanna come with us? Caleb's taking Greta on a picnic. We're going along to fish."

"Does Caleb know you're joining them?" Polly gave her little cousin an amused look.

"My daddy and Uncle Giddy said we could!" He raced away.

Trying hard not to laugh, Polly pressed her lips together.

"Why"—the doctor swiped the bucket from her hand—"do I have the feeling Caleb's not going to be thrilled with this development?"

Losing the battle, Polly laughed aloud. "If I don't miss my guess, Greta's mother is probably packing enough food for an army and will send her two youngest along, too. Greta and Caleb are both eighteen. Both families feel it's a good match, but it wouldn't hurt for them to wait a few years before meeting at the altar."

"Being an only child suddenly is far more appealing to me. When I decide to woo a young woman, I won't have tagalongs."

Is he thinking of courting someone? Polly felt a twinge at the thought, then got angry at herself. *Well, Uncle Bryce couldn't be more wrong—it's certainly not me. He'll want a meek, mild woman who stays home. We'd never suit.* Reaching around, she pulled her apron strings and retied them looser.

sixteen

"I'll have to ask you to be careful to stay on the path, Doctor." Polly set out at a brisk pace. "It's pretty narrow, but we rely on each plant."

"Sure." His stride matched hers until he stepped ahead to open the garden gate.

Polly walked into the garden and caught sight of Uncle Bryce glowering from the barn. She'd reassure him later that the doctor had come for professional reasons. "The garden is divided into two sections." She headed toward the right. "Though most of these herbs can be medicinal, their major use is in cooking."

"Interesting."

Walking along, Polly named the plants aloud: "Rosemary, thyme, sage, basil, sweet and wild marjoram, chives, lovage, lemon balm, parsley, borage, mint, fennel—"

"Fennel is effective for dyspepsia."

Polly nodded and started using her knife to cut small bits of fennel. "True, but I'm harvesting it because I'm making a brine for pickles. Dill, fennel, a little onion, and mustard make for tasty pickles."

"You don't have any mustard here."

She looked around the patch. "No need to. It grows wild all around the area. I used mustard in the poultices for the Greene children."

He nodded. "I keep a fair supply of dried mustard on hand."

Well, that was nice. He just admitted that we sometimes use the same curative. Maybe we'll find other things we can agree upon.

She dropped more fennel into the pail. "Let's go to the other half. It holds the medicinals. Mama and Aunt Delilah put in a lot of work to plant things that were scarce or foreign to this region."

"So am I to presume you keep cuttings from plants that are out of season in that room over there?" He gestured toward the hallway between her cabin and her parents' abode.

"Those are the things we've harvested and keep on hand. Mama and I gather almost daily."

"I haven't found the people of Reliable to be of such poor health." He followed her steps with caution along the narrow path between patches of plants as he continued to discuss the citizenry. "On average, I think they're actually rather hale."

Polly glanced back and noted how his footsteps literally overlaid hers. He'd been walking precisely where she had—a mark of his respect for her precious garden. Gratitude filled her heart.

"Do you disagree? Have you considered your neighbors to be sickly?"

"No, no. Not at all. It's that you never know when you'll need something, so Mama and I have been diligent to keep stock on hand. I noticed your shelves when we put that plaster on Cal. At the time, I remember thinking your supply rivaled one of the pharmacies in San Francisco."

"The mayor told me Reliable didn't have a pharmacy, so I planned on having to dispense whatever I prescribed."

"That'll be handy. In the past, if we didn't have something, we sent to San Francisco. Waiting is hard—that's why the garden here keeps growing. We've added something nearly every year."

He scanned the collection. "I recognize the feverfew."

"Tansy's on this side of it. St. John's wort is on the other side. Then we have comfrey, herb Robert, self-heal, valerian—"

"Did you try valerian for your headaches?"

"Yes, but to no avail." She gave him a sideways look. "My headaches are not from nerves."

"I didn't mean to imply they were. Valerian can be effective for a variety of problems."

"It's putting down good roots—roots are what we harvest. But you only dig them up in September." She felt her nose wrinkle. "They don't smell bad fresh, but once they're dried, they reek."

"So how can you keep them in that shed by your cabin?"

"We dry them in the barn. After grinding them up and putting them in a tightly stoppered jar, the smell is contained. It's useful for insomnia and women's complaints." The minute the words slipped out of her mouth, Polly wanted to spin around and flee.

Doc didn't bat an eye. "Lydia Pinkham's Vegetable Compound contains cohosh and more than twenty percent alcohol." He leaned over and examined wood betony as he added, "Several women partake of it."

"Mama says cohosh is good, but we don't add any spirits to our elixirs."

The doctor nodded. "Good, good."

She didn't want to continue the discussion of women's complaints. As healers, they both dealt with such issues, and the Bible even spoke about Christ healing a woman with a female complaint, but it didn't seem like a proper subject of conversation. Grabbing the opportunity he'd opened, Polly said, "That plant you're inspecting is wood betony. It can be helpful with mouth sores and throat irritations."

"Fascinating. Do you mind if I take samples?"

Extending her gathering knife to him, she said, "Not at all."

They spent time going from plant to plant. Doc asked several questions and made interesting observations. As it became awkward for him to harvest, label the small papers in which he folded the sample, and tuck them into his pocket, Polly took back her knife and assisted him. She used the techniques Mama taught her.

The doctor questioned her every action. "I use the petals that are darkest because they are richest in the healing properties. . . ." "The leaves are best when harvested in morning shade, so we won't take any today. . . ." "These must be rinsed thrice before drying upside down. . . ."

He scribbled notes to himself and asked dozens and dozens of questions. Polly surprised herself with just how much Mama had taught her. The teaching had been so gradual, she never fully appreciated the lore Mama shared so generously.

At one point, the doctor frowned. "Why aren't you wearing a bonnet out here?"

She lifted a hand and touched her hair. *Oh, dear me. It's probably a horrible mess.* Self-conscious laughter bubbled out of her.

"I didn't mean to embarrass you. My only thought was that sunlight might trigger headaches."

"I love the sunshine."

"Hey there, Doc." Mama leaned over the fence. Try as she might, she didn't manage to disguise the grimace of pain that came with the action. "Nice of you to drop by. Why don't you stay to lunch?"

"I'd be honored." He sidestepped between a few plants very carefully and lowered his voice. "I'd also be honored if you'd allow me to examine your back. Something must be done."

Mama let out a chortle. "Oh, Doc, now if that wasn't smooth

as rain off a winderpane. I've done my share of bargainin' folks into accepting care. Suppose it's justice someone turned the tables on me."

Doc dusted off his hands. "How long 'til lunch?"

"We have time for you to check on her now," Polly said. She didn't want to give Mama an opportunity to come up with an excuse and wiggle out of an examination. Knowing Mama, Polly figured that's exactly what she'd do, too.

She couldn't fault Doc's bedside manner. He'd washed his hands outside while she helped Mama change into a lawn nightdress. Once he came in, Doc performed a deft examination of Mama's back, asked several pertinent questions, and managed to be both professional and personable.

"The hot and cold packs and the liniment are all fine. Continue on with those and the massages," he told Polly. "I'd like to try traction—a series of ropes and weights to stretch the spine." He held his fists together, side to side, then slowly drew them apart. "Slow, gentle force could straighten the kink and allow the nerves and disc to slip into a natural position again."

"Mama, that ought to work!"

Mama sighed. "Hope so. You jest tell us what to do, Doc."

"I'll step out and talk to your husband about rigging up the traction apparatus."

He left, and Lovejoy tugged on Polly's hand. "Help me get dressed. I wanna soak up some sunshine this noon afore he and yore Daddy strap me to the bed."

Slender and sprightly, Mama had never needed to resort to stays, but since her back started paining her, Polly had made her a back binding with boning in it to render some support. She laced it up, then knelt to help Mama with her shoes while Mama buttoned up her day gown. Once they were done, Polly opened the door, and Mama gingerly stepped outside.

Lord, let Doctor Walcott's treatment work. Mama's hurting. I just want her to be well again.

Doc stood over by Daddy and some of the boys. Daddy's brows were furrowed.

"Yore daddy and uncles are good men," Mama whispered to Polly as they headed toward the tables. "Don't you be troublin' yourself o'er how things'll work out. They're not gonna give Doc a hard time or carry a grudge. Feelin' ran high t'other day, but I know 'em—they'll be examples. A shining example is a better lesson than a lot of gusty words."

Polly wasn't quite so sure. Then again, since Mama let Doc examine her, that ought to mean a lot to Daddy. Then, too, Doc had accepted the lunch invitation, so they'd be breaking bread together.

A few moments later, Doc, Daddy, and Uncle Paul strode up with an odd assortment of ropes, leather, and—"That can't be the pulley from the hayloft!" Polly couldn't hide her astonishment.

"I scrubbed it," Uncle Paul confirmed.

"Let's go," Daddy said to Mama.

Mama's jaw jutted forward in a stubborn tilt. "I'm aimin' to eat first."

"That'll be fine." Doc nodded. "It's not healthy for you to lie in one place for days on end. I want you to be up for half an hour, four times a day." He then tacked on, "But no working during that time. It's just for eating and essentials."

Mama gave him an exasperated look.

Polly laughed. "Mama, your face has the same expression as the Greene children when I tell them they need those stinky mustard and onion poultices!"

"I'd rather wear a poultice and still be upright," Mama muttered. She glanced at the doctor. "Don't you fret yoreself none. I git het up when a patient doesn't mind me. I'll be good and foller yore instructions."

"Thank you," he said in a tone that sounded mildly amused.

At lunch, the doctor sat at the lunch table by Polly's side. That was saying plenty since there were six tables and he could have plopped down wherever he wanted. Maybe he was avoiding April, though. The girls had come back from visiting Beulah and gone in to prepare lunch. April got news that Doc was there, dashed out of the kitchen, and immediately started making a pest of herself.

Uncle Gideon stood at a table and clapped his hands once. Everyone fell silent for the prayer. "Our Lord of abundance and grace, we give thanks for Your providence. Bless and keep us as we seek to do Your will, and we ask a special touch of healing for our Lovejoy. Amen."

❧

Every second or third day for the next two weeks, Dr. Walcott came out to check on Mama, go on a gathering walk with Polly, and sit beside her at the lunch table. Mama's improvement pleased them all, and Polly looked forward to his visits.

They wandered along the back path toward a stand of trees. Polly gently tugged on Doc's shirtsleeve. "Beware of that plant hanging off the far tree. It's poison oak."

"It doesn't look like any poison oak I've ever seen. Are you sure?"

"Aunt Miriam found out the hard way." Polly stood on tiptoe to peel off a little bark from a neighboring tree.

"What is that for?"

"Kate wants to tan a little leather. This'll do the trick, and if she adds a little iron salt, the leather will go black." She stuffed the bark into her gathering bag. "But don't tell Uncle Titus. She's making him a belt as a surprise for his birthday."

"Why doesn't she just buy stain?"

"Then he'd find out about it. With such a big family, it's hard to keep secrets. We help one another out."

He peeled off more bark. "How much do you need?"

"Just a little more." . . . *Of the bark. But a lot more of you.*

❧

Eric thoroughly enjoyed Polly's companionship. Such a bright woman! Clever, cheerful, hardworking. He'd never met anyone with such a capacity to love. Her family, neighbors, folks in town—even the animals on the ranch—they all adored her.

And I do, too. Eric halted midmotion at that realization. He'd told himself he was interested in Polly because of her abilities, her knowledge, even her slightly quirky ways. But the truth stared back at him. He'd come to make peace with her and explore her knowledge of plants, but somewhere on one of their walks, she'd gathered his heart just as surely as anything else she collected.

seventeen

Lovejoy's back improved almost daily. In a matter of another week or so, she wouldn't require traction at all. Eric had been collecting botanical specimens with Polly out of interest—but that interest was every bit as much personal as it was scientific. The time had come to test the waters to see if she returned any feelings for him. He'd couch it carefully in such a way that they'd still be able to bump into one another if she tactfully indicated her affections lay elsewhere.

He'd never seen her walking or riding with anyone. She never sat at church with a young man or appeared at the mercantile with anyone other than family—unless he counted the MacPherson boys, and they were distant kin. The fact that no man had yet managed to capture her heart both puzzled and pleased Eric. Lord willing, he'd be that man.

I'll offer to bring my microscope and equipment here to Chance Ranch. Flushed with excitement over that idea, he said, "I've been conducting experiments on the plants you and I have been gathering together. Perhaps I could do some of the experiments here at your ranch as the season starts to change. The last few days, you've mentioned autumn harvesting will begin. Maybe I could accompany you, and then we could prepare powders and slides."

"Aunt Delilah doodles with her colored pencils every chance she has. If you'd like, she'd probably illustrate your notes."

"Great!" Delilah's talent would be an asset, but she also stuck close to her smaller son and the house. That meant

143

her sketching wouldn't involve her tagging along while he conducted his wooing. He still remembered how the Chances sent a few of the younger boys along on Caleb's picnic as chaperones. A few times, April or Kate had come along on the gathering walks, but neither seemed especially thrilled with all of the botanical conversation. Thereafter, they found excuses not to tag along—which pleased Eric to no end.

Heading back toward the ranch house, feeling confident in all he and Polly had accomplished, Eric continued, "I'd like to work with you more, train you with some of my things."

"Like the special Johnson & Johnson plaster?"

"Yes. . ." He paused, then dared to push on, "and like childbirth." *If you become my wife, we'll tend women together.*

Polly stopped and gave him an entertained look. "In eighteen years, Mama's lost only two women in this township within the first ten days of their deliveries. Can you boast the same statistic?"

"We both know I haven't practiced for eighteen years, Polly. I do have modern scientific techniques." Though confident in his own medical ability, his assurance of Polly's faith in his talent flagged. Perhaps she wasn't attracted to him, either. He'd come too far to back out, though. "The pastor's wife is due any day now, and—"

"She's been clear about her desires, Doctor. Mama and I will be attending her."

"Your mother oughtn't do that. It's too hard for her yet. I thought you and I—"

Polly's eyes widened. "How could you suggest that? Mrs. Abrams already told you how she feels. I'm not going to plow over her feelings."

"She's older—far older—than most first-time mothers. Complications are more common in such circumstances." He could see he wasn't getting anywhere. Eric heaved a sigh. "Then promise me two things, Polly: that you'll summon me if there are any problems whatsoever, and that you'll use my ergot."

"You insisted on your ergot at Beulah's delivery, too. Why?"

"Because..." He looked at Polly and hated to crush her confidence, but the folklore she used was still dangerous. He needed to convince her to use sound medicinals, even if he couldn't win her heart. "Because ergot is scientifically proven to prevent postpartum hemorrhage. The rust scrapings and rye whiskey you use are hazardous to the patient."

"Rust scrapings and rye whiskey," Polly echoed. Her blue eyes grew huge, and her mouth dropped open. Laughter bubbled out of her. "Rust scrapings and rye whiskey? Oh, Doctor. The whiskey on the table was to sterilize it. By the time I arrived, Eunice was ready to deliver. I didn't have time to do a lye soap scrub. As for rust—you misunderstood. We have Hattie send us scrapings of rusty rye."

"And my ergot is from rye," he said. He chortled in disbelief and relief.

"Oh, my." She laughed merrily. "Between that and the ax at a birthing, no wonder you felt Mama and I were quacks!"

"When I was just five, my mother died in childbirth, Polly. It's one of the reasons I became a physician. Attending Reliable's women during that dangerous time is important—for them and to me."

Polly looked him in the eye and slowly shook her head. "I love delivering babies and helping the mamas, too, but that's not the issue. The fact is, women have the right to decide who's going to help them. I'm not going to sway a woman to come see me if she seeks you out; you oughtn't do the reverse."

Stubborn woman. Eric looked at her in silence.

"You suggested partnering. If a woman wants the both of

us there, I'm fine with that. Mama always said another pair of skilled hands isn't ever wasted."

Eric couldn't deny that fact. Nonetheless, he didn't want Polly carrying on the misguided notion that she could cure the collective ills of Reliable's citizens. "As I mentioned, it would be a good thing for me to train you in modern medical practices."

"The traction you set up for Mama works beautifully. Those kinds of things fascinate me. I'd enjoy learning whatever you're willing to teach me."

"Good." Maybe things could work out, after all. *Why does she have to be so confusing?*

She slanted him a look. "I'm willing to assist you, too—in regular cases, emergencies, and during surgical procedures. Please feel free to send for me."

He studied her. Something about the attentiveness in her posture—the slight forward tilt of her head and the ever-so-subtle narrowing of her eyes—made him take notice. "Are you referring to a specific case, Polly?"

"Might be."

Eric frowned.

She shifted subtly. If it weren't for the way her skirt scuffed a tiny mark in the earth, he would have missed it entirely. "Oh, dear." She winced. "This is difficult. With Mama, I'm free to discuss the neighbors to whom we render care. On the other hand, it's not right for me to reveal things to you about them. I'm afraid it's going to be problematic."

"There are bound to be difficulties. You and I agree on something, though: The patient's welfare is always foremost."

Her eyes pled with him for confirmation. "I referred someone to you yesterday."

"Is that so? No one's sent for me or come to the clinic."

The pleasure that she'd sent a case to him couldn't offset the concern he felt. Polly still felt competent treating simple cases; this one must be exceptionally involved or difficult.

Polly started toward the barnyard. Eric strode alongside her, matching her rapid pace. The resolute set of her jaw warned him something was wrong. "What is it?"

"I suppose that partnership's going to be trial by fire." She dropped the gathering sack onto a table and called, "Hey, in the barn!"

Someone stuck out his head. Eric thought it might be Tanner.

"Saddle up Blossom right away!"

"Where're you going?"

"The Big G." Polly looked at Eric. "I'll grab my satchel. Did you bring your doctor's bag?"

"Yes."

"Good." She headed into her parents' cabin. Eric stood in the doorway and overheard her whisper, "Mama, I'm taking Doc over to the Big G. Mr. Garcia didn't go get checked."

"Mmm. Best you shake a leg. I didn't like the way he looked."

Polly headed into the odd closetlike place. Eric invited himself to go see what she was gathering from the shelves.

To his surprise, the shelves weren't dusty—they were all painted a grayish brown. The jars, jugs, and bottles were all sparkling clean and bore labels. Sure, bunches of leaves and roots hanging from pegs pounded into the roof looked strange. He suspected there was some order or method to the arrangement, but this wasn't the time to ascertain those details.

"What are you getting?"

"Essentials. If it's what I think it is, we'll take him to your office for surgery; if it's worsened, you might have to operate at his place." Metal pieces chinked together as she lifted a tightly wrapped towel and stuffed it into her satchel. "I'll bring my instruments just in case."

"Fine." He grabbed a bar of lye soap.

She took a bottle of carbolic acid and the accompanying mister, a container of tincture of iodine, then one last bottle and slipped them all into her satchel.

He couldn't believe what he'd seen on the label. "You have ether?"

"Yes." Right beside where that bottle had rested on the shelf sat paper-and-cotton cones in which to drip the ether. That surprised him; most often, folks saturated a sponge with it, but many didn't awaken after the surgery because the anesthesia went too deep.

"A doctor in San Francisco trained Mama and me about it. He suggested the cone because he's seen too many people harmed with an ether sponge."

"Polly, why don't you tell me what you've diagnosed?"

She stopped for a moment and gave him a grave look. "I suspect appendicitis."

Grabbing her wrist in one hand and the satchel in the other, he plowed toward the door. His voice vibrated with concern and supplication as he prayed, "God help us all."

eighteen

The sickly sweet smell of ether lingered in the kitchen as Polly carefully washed the instruments. As Doc came back into the room, she asked, "How is he?"

"I got him settled in bed. Pulse is strong, breathing is steady. He's in God's hands now."

Polly nodded. When they'd arrived, they'd found Mr. Garcia in his stable. He lay doubled up beside his saddle, barely conscious. Doc hefted him, carried him into the two-room shack, and gave the shambled place a look of despair.

Polly hastily swept everything off the table, and in a moment of tension, Doc still managed some mirth. "No time for a lye scrub. Do you think he has any of that medicinal whiskey for sterilizing the table?"

Polly located a bottle and doused the table thoroughly, and that was where they operated. The water in the stove reservoir was still scalding, so she'd been able to give the instruments a cursory dip for better sterility. They'd worked furiously but well together. Polly paused from washing those instruments now, glanced up at the doctor, and nodded. "Yes, it's up to the Lord now."

He watched her as she washed the handles of a pair of hemostats. Suddenly, Polly felt unaccountably shy. She concentrated on making sure the little metal ridges on the other end of the instrument came sparkling clean.

"You did the right thing, Polly. If we hadn't arrived when we did, that appendix would have ruptured and Mr. Garcia would have died. It would have been a lonely, painful death."

She nodded. "Healing is a matter of asking God's guidance and doing your best. I'm glad you were here. I couldn't have operated."

"We work exceptionally well together." Doc dipped each of the just-washed instruments into boiling water, then set them on a clean towel. "I'm not sure what's yours and what's mine."

Polly stared at the shiny collection of scissors, probes, retractors, hemostats, scalpels, and needles. "Yours are the experienced ones. Most of mine don't see much use. Other than births and doing sutures, I don't even take them from their sterile wraps."

"Your plants are your tools."

His words left her feeling lightheaded with pleasure. Polly leaned against the sink. "Yes, they are."

Doc frowned, wrapped his hand around her elbow, and dragged her toward a chair. "Here. Sit down." As soon as he'd deposited her in the seat, he opened the door and muttered to himself, "I was an idiot not to air out the room."

"Really, I'm fine."

He came over, tilted her face to his, and shook his head. "Ether is harsh. You're—"

"If you dare call me fragile, I might never forgive you." Even though she didn't feel weak, she didn't mind his touch. It made her feel. . .cared for.

His brows hiked upward, and he let out a short laugh. "The fresh air is giving you back your sass. As for you not forgiving me. . ." He stroked his thumb slowly across her jaw. "You don't carry grudges. If you did, I wouldn't be standing here."

"Why are you standing there?" Uncle Bryce's voice made them both turn toward the door. A thunderous scowl darkened his face. "I thought somebody was supposed to be sick. And you"—he shook his forefinger at her—"Polly Chance, you know better. You're not to go gallivanting off without one of us comin' along."

"It was an emergency, and I was with Polly." Doc stood beside her.

Uncle Bryce didn't respond verbally. He gave Polly a we'll-talk-about-this-later look.

"Mr. Garcia's going to need help for a while here." Polly tried to steer the conversation into safer territory. "Could you please go to the MacPhersons and see if they can spare Peter and Matt? I'll ask Cal and Tanner to come, too."

"From the looks of things, it'll take the four of them weeks to whip this place into shape." Uncle Bryce folded his arms and continued to wear a stubborn expression. "You can tell plenty about a man from his animals. Garcia's stable is full of beasts he's ignored."

"He's been sick, Uncle Bryce. Really sick." She refused to divulge the nature of the malady, and her uncle knew better than to ask particulars, but Polly did impart, "We just operated. How about if you and I go water and feed those animals while Dr. Walcott checks in on Mr. Garcia?"

"So you're done here?"

"Not yet."

"I aim to toss you back on Blossom and send you home. Ain't fittin' for a young woman to be all on her own out in the wilds with two men."

Heat flashed from her bosom to her hairline. Polly wanted to let out a squawk of outrage. Uncle Bryce had no call to be embarrassing her like this. "Mama knew Dr. Walcott and I were paying a medical call. No one will give it another thought."

"Your mama couldn't concoct a bad thought about anybody," Uncle Bryce grumbled. "Don't hold her up as a sample on how others think."

"More's the pity," the doctor said. "I've found Lovejoy to be a wonderful Christian example."

Uncle Bryce shook his finger at Doc. "An example. Yes, a Christian example. There you have it." He paused a moment, then blurted out, "Actually, you don't, and that's the problem."

Doc's lips parted. He waited a heartbeat, then asked solemnly, "Have I offended you or someone?"

"You wander off, missy." Uncle Bryce shot Polly a "mind-me" look.

She lifted her chin. "The doctor asked a question. You made an accusation in front of me, and he deserves the opportunity to clear his name."

Folding his arms across his chest, Uncle Bryce glowered at Dr. Walcott. "You've been to the Nugget." He paused meaningfully and cast a quick glance at Polly. "Now you walk off, missy."

"There's no need," the doctor said.

Uncle Bryce shook his head. "I tried to handle this best as I could. Neither of you is making it easy. Fact is, Doc, it's known you've been upstairs at the Nugget."

"Yes, I have," Doc said mildly. He looked from Polly to Uncle Bryce and back again. He didn't sound in the least bit offended or defensive. "I treat anyone in need. Where they live or what they do for a living isn't an issue for me."

"Folks get the wrong impression," Uncle Bryce grumbled.

"I suppose that could be true. But Jesus didn't ask what people did for a living; He reached out and healed them. I won't do any different. If folks make false judgments about me, that's their business. I'm accountable to the Lord."

"You're right," Polly murmured.

"Reckon so," Uncle Bryce agreed in a surly tone.

Doc asked, "Is there anything else?"

"Not at all," she said swiftly before Uncle Bryce set in for a repeat of his opinion. He tended to do that. Stubborn as a mule, he'd likely prod the doc just to be sure he'd gotten the whole truth. Polly felt certain in her heart the doctor had been completely, wholly honest.

"Then I'll go check on our patient, Polly." Doc headed across the cabin.

Polly accompanied her uncle out to the stable. She half-stomped out there, then turned on him once they were out of earshot from the cabin. "What got into you?"

"I oughta be asking you that selfsame question. I told you right from the start to beware of that man and not go off alone with him. That first time he came to wander 'round and gawk at your plants, I warned you not to keep company with him. The man keeps turning up like a plague of flies."

"He's not a pest; he's a professional. Not one single thing's passed between us that is in the least bit questionable."

"Keep it thataway." Bryce started watering the animals. "Soon as we feed these critters, I want you to go back home. He don't care what folks think, but you need to. What he does still reflects on you if you keep company together."

Polly thrust the scoop into the oats and yanked it back out. Uncle Bryce tended to be an easygoing man, but when he dug in his heels, he could teach stubborn to a mule. She'd have to talk to Daddy and have him set his little brother straight.

❧

Pastor Abe stood at the pulpit and beamed at the congregation. "I'd like to open the service with a special praise. The Lord blessed my wife and me with a healthy little boy late last evening. Given the fact that we've waited for him for so long, he's to be called Isaac."

The rest of the parishioners laughed and murmured at the

wonderful news and clever name. Eric forced a smile. He'd been home last night, but no one sought his assistance. The woman he loved essentially had stolen away the part of medical practice he most enjoyed.

Daniel Chance scooted into the pew beside Eric. He gave him a curt nod, then paid attention to the pastor. Well, he tried to. The man fidgeted. He curled his hands around the seat on each side of his thighs in a death grip, then eased back and drummed his fingers on the edge. A moment later, he twisted and leaned closer. "Meet me outside."

nineteen

Eric rose and followed him out to the churchyard. "Is there a problem?"

"Lovejoy's back is bad again. She went to help the pastor's wife last night. Polly gave her something to stop the spasms and help her sleep, but I don't like this one bit. The traction— I rigged it up the way you showed me, but all it did was make Lovejoy hurt worse."

"I'll go check on her. Why don't you ask the congregation to pray?" Eric didn't wait for a response. He unhitched his gelding and swung up into the saddle. The road to Chance Ranch would take half an hour—far longer than he'd accept. Eric cut across a patch of land, jumped the fence, and took the most direct route.

Polly opened the cabin door as his horse skidded to a halt. "Dr. Walcott!"

"Your father sent me." He dismounted and headed into the cabin. "He said your mother's in a bad way."

Polly shut the door behind him, and a vile odor permeated the cabin. "I just rubbed her down with liniment."

"I'm tellin' you, Doc," Lovejoy said from the bed, "hit's a case of wonderin' if the cure's worse'n the affliction. McCleans Volcanic liniment reeks to high heaven, don't it?"

"Does it make you feel better?" He bent over the bed and noticed the lines of pain bracketing her mouth.

"Reckon I couldn't feel any worse." She sighed. " 'Tis my own fault, too. I been fightin' the direction God's leadin' me.

155

He knocked me on my back so's I'd be forced to look up."

"Then I'm going to tie you up to the traction and keep you here until you and God get that matter ironed out." He assessed her, then looked at Polly. "I need to apply traction higher on the back than we did before. Instead of the waist belt, we'll need to devise something that straps just beneath her arms."

Polly looked around the cabin.

Lovejoy winced from a spasm. "Cain't we jest use a belt?"

"If we rigged cloth into a suspenderlike arrangement in the back, that would work." Eric headed for the open door to the apothecary. "Don't you keep the cotton bandaging material in here?"

"Grosgrain ribbon would be stronger and flatter. I'm sure Laurel has yards of it in her sewing basket." Polly slipped past him and opened the door that led to the adjoining cabin.

The only time he'd been inside her cabin was when she had the migraine. Other than a vague memory of the floral scent and white furniture, Eric didn't remember anything about the place since he'd been focused on Polly's headache. Curious about where Polly lived with her cousins, Eric craned his neck and took in the yellow gingham curtains, the bright rag rug, and the far wall that bore a large wreath of dried flowers and a picture. The place looked like it belonged to Polly—cheery and practical.

She called over her shoulder, "The boys' cabin is next door. There's a box under the bunk bed on the left that holds clothes they've outgrown and can pass on. Could you please go see if there's a belt?"

"Sure." Eric walked into the cabin she specified and headed toward the box. He had to step over discarded socks, a book, and a shirt and push aside a saddle frame. They'd added on to the cabin in order to accommodate what looked to be another set of bunk beds, and the sheer disorder of a bunch of young men gave the cabin an air of rowdy acceptance.

For a moment, Eric looked about and felt a pang. He'd missed out on all of this—the sense of belonging, of having a brother as a confidant, of scuffling and arguing and teasing with someone. He envied the Chance men for having brothers and sons so they'd never sit alone at a table and eat in deafening silence.

Setting aside those thoughts, Eric yanked a crate from beneath the bed and rummaged through it. He found a belt he thought might work and jogged back to join Polly at Lovejoy's bedside.

It took a few tries before they devised a setup Eric felt would work. He bent over Lovejoy. "I'm going to lift you so Polly can slip the strap beneath you."

"How's about I wind my arms 'bout your neck and pull myself up?"

"Mama, you're going to hurt Dr. Walcott's feelings. He'll get the impression you don't think he's strong enough."

Eric flashed Polly a smile. She'd kept him from having to argue with Lovejoy and managed to hint that she found his physique manly.

"Okay. Let's get on with it."

A ragged moan tore through Lovejoy's throat as Eric lifted her. He murmured wordless sounds of comfort, then carefully laid her back down once Polly arranged the apparatus. Quickly, he buckled the belt, then attached the weights to form the traction. "Her muscles are already in spasm. I want to go ahead and get this done so she won't have to endure another jolt," he said to Polly.

Her hands shook, but she hastily tied the weights as he'd shown her the last time. Once done, she darted to the other side of the bed and wiped away Lovejoy's tears. "I'm sorry, Mama.

It'll be better soon. Jesus loves you and cares about your pain. You know He does."

Eric watched Polly. Her hands were beautiful—caring, gentle, soothing. She moved with grace that never hinted that there was any urgency in her actions. Tiny things—pushing back a wisp of hair, fluffing a pillow, speaking in a soft, confident tone—everything she did exuded love. She gave her heart to each patient. He'd seen her this way with Beulah, Perry, the Greene children, and during the surgery. Her herbs, teas, and poultices might well have medicinal effects, but the real secret behind her healing was that she simply opened her heart to the Lord and let Him pour His love through her.

After ten agonizing minutes, Lovejoy's body relaxed. She closed her eyes as her head sank deeper into the pillow. "Confession's good for the soul. I need to make a confession. My pride's gotten in the way of my common sense."

"Mama, you don't need to—"

"Child, I do. 'Member how I told you healin' ain't just flesh and bone? When somethin' ails a body, a heavy soul makes it worse. I gotta speak my piece here."

"All right, Mama." Polly curled her hand around her mother's.

Eric wondered if he ought to leave. Was this a mother-daughter moment? He didn't do well with these family things—the nuances escaped him.

"Doc, stop bein' antsy as a turkey at Thanksgivin'. Ain't nothin' sweeter than God's children sharin' their joys and woes. I seen you plenty these last months. God claims you as one of His own. I ain't feelin' shy 'bout openin' my heart in front of you."

"I'm honored."

Polly glanced up at him. He couldn't read the look in her eyes.

Lovejoy let out a long, choppy breath. "Of all the things I like, catchin' babies always pleases me most. 'Tis a miracle, and the both of you know what I mean. Mayhap, on account I couldn't have me babes of my own, I came to think of midwivin' as being God's way of lettin' me have a snippet of that joy.

"I niver thought I'd have me a man who cherished me or little girls who called me their ma. God ended up givin' me my Dan'l and Polly and Ginny Mae. But sometimes God gives us things for a season. Ginny Mae was here just awhile; then the dear Lord called her home."

Eric watched as the two women's touch altered—the hold tightened in remembered grief. They'd shared that loss together. *What would it be like to have someone to bear the burden of sorrow with you?* His father had sent him away when his mother died. His grandparents had passed on at the same time. He'd never known the solace of mourning along with others who'd felt that deep wound of loss.

"You were the only mama Ginny Mae ever knew, and she adored you. God blessed us the day you marched onto the ranch."

Lovejoy managed a weak laugh. "Yore papa shore didn't think so at the start. But that all worked out. Our love is one of God's gifts. He's been generous to me. I enjoyed bein' a healer; then I even got to share that with my Pollywog. All those times, they fill my heart like a treasure box. Any smart woman would count herself blessed and let it be. Only I ain't been so smart.

"After that horse kicked me last year, I knew I couldn't keep on doin' everything. Dan'l and me—we talked it over, and he's the one who told the mayor to put that ad out for a town doctor. We prayed o'er the man God would send. Yup, Doc, afore you come, my Dan'l and me done covered you in 'nuff prayers to keep a whole passel of angels busy."

"I'm humbled." *Oh, am I humbled. These people saw a need,*

provided a job for me, and set up my clinic. I thought I had to prove myself, and they'd already accepted me. I stood on my pride and challenged them.

"But you got here, and 'stead of me letting go, I didn't. I held on. Oh, I reasoned it through—but that's not what God asked of me. He told me to let go and trust Him to use the both of you to do His healin' works. Me? I figured I could sorta help and partner and dabble. Not a soul knew it—but I did. Deep in my heart, I did."

You're not the only one who's been guilty of that. I was so sure of myself, I didn't seek God's guidance as I should have.

"So here I am, flat on my back, and it's time for me to come clean. Dan'l learned a hard lesson early in his life, and he favors a sayin' that's fitting. Nothin' ever stays the same, but the changes are always for better if we give 'em to God."

"Daddy is fond of saying that, isn't he?"

"Yup. Hit's time I stopped tryin' to force God into seein' things my way and I look at things through His eyes. My season of bein' a healer is over. I 'spect it ain't gonna be easy for me to turn loose, but now that you heard me out, you cain hold me accountable."

Silence and the pungent smell of liniment hovered in the air.

"Mama, I'll do my best to trust the Lord and care for folks." Polly laced her fingers with her mother's. Such a simple move—but it connected them, twined them together in an unconscious move that bespoke the intimacy of their bond. "I think you're right. God sent Doc here, and we can handle things. From now on, you can concentrate on getting better and spoiling Daddy."

Longing to be a part of Polly's world where caring came so easily, Eric dared to rest his right hand on her shoulder. She didn't pull away. Instead, she looked up at him and gave him that smile that made his heart skip a beat.

He'd wondered if he'd ever find a time and way to apologize for how he'd acted toward Polly and her mother. Polly acted as if he'd never once overstepped himself, but that was a tribute to her character. Lovejoy was right—nothing was better than honesty among believers.

Eric cleared his throat. "Since humble pie is on the menu, I'm going to have to eat a slice, too—a big slice."

twenty

"Grab you a fork, son." Lovejoy gave him an unsteady grin. "We won't make it taste too bad."

"I came here thinking book knowledge and scientific treatments were what it took to heal. As a Christian, I knew God is the Great Physician, but I let pride get ahead of wisdom. Daniel is an astute man. He nailed me on it, and I've had to do a lot of thinking and praying. My only pride ought to be in Christ's works."

"Iff'n my back weren't so nasty, I'd be standin' and shoutin' glory, 'cuz God is faithful to meet us at our honest needs."

"I haven't had a very meek spirit," Polly said.

"Never did," Lovejoy shot back. "But your vine bears fruit of other kinds."

"It does, indeed." Eric looked at Polly and recited, "Love, joy, peace, longsuffering, gentleness—"

Polly and her mother started laughing.

Baffled, Eric demanded, "What's so funny?"

A look of tenderness crossed Lovejoy's face. "My mama loved that verse in Ephesians."

"In fact, she named her daughters after it," Polly tacked on.

"Lovejoy," Eric said slowly, "and your sister is Temperance."

"Mama used all but Longsuffering and Meekness."

"I've been sitting in church worrying about you, woman." Daniel Chance strode in. "And here you are, reciting your family tree."

"Betwixt Polly rubbing me down and dosing me up and the

doc roping me like this, I'm tolerable."

Daniel knelt by the bed and kissed her. "Listening to that, you sound like a seasoned roast on a spit!"

Polly moved out of the way and laughed.

"We prayed for you this morning," Daniel said.

"Thankee, Dan'l. We've had us our own time with Jesus here."

"I'll go rustle up some Sunday supper." Polly headed for the door.

"No, no." Her father shook his head.

Eric wondered if Daniel would make any reference to his daughter's lack of culinary skill. He'd been understandably protective of her in other matters.

"It's family picnic day," Daniel went on to say. "I'll slap together sandwiches for your mama and me. You go on ahead."

"I was so worried about Mama, I forgot."

Eric couldn't recall any announcement at church about a picnic. Had he been out on a call?

Lovejoy called, "Doc, I'm shore you oughta go, too. Us and the MacPhersons git together for Sunday picnic 'bout once a month or so. Since we both got our boys up at Mr. Garcia's place, Eunice sent word that we'd hold the picnic up there. Thataway, the boys cain all show off their hard work, and Mr. Garcia'll git up and walk outside and eat more. You've been payin' calls on him since you done surgery—'tis 'bout time you broke bread with the man to show him you think he's hale again."

Daniel came out onto the porch, and Eric discussed how often Lovejoy's traction could be removed. Polly disappeared and returned with Blossom saddled.

"Thanks for coming, Doc. That traction had me puzzled. It made Lovejoy a heap better last time," Daniel said.

"It'll help again, but she needs to be careful. No more lifting or straining for her."

"We'll find other things to keep her busy." Dan grinned at him. "Things have worked out better than I thought with you." Daniel shook his hand. "Glad you came."

"Thanks. I'm glad I'm here." He stepped off the porch, wrapped his hands around Polly's waist, and lifted her into the saddle. For the few minutes when he had hold of her, everything felt so right. *More than anything, she's why I'm glad I'm here.*

❧

Showing up at the family picnic with the doc earned Polly plenty of sly smiles and assessing looks. Her cousins sometimes brought along the folks they fancied. Caleb and Greta walked by, then Johnna and Trevor. No one was giving either pair a second glance.

Polly couldn't decide what she wanted. *Well, yes, I can. I want Doc to court me. But until I clear things with April and he makes a move, it's going to be downright embarrassing for everyone to keep gawking. I never should have come.*

Doc dismounted, and Polly decided to scramble down before he might feel obligated to help her. With his fine manners, he was always doing chivalrous things—but that would fan speculation among the family.

"I need to go fetch something." Doc smiled. "Please go ahead and eat. I'll be back later."

April scurried up. "Doctor!"

"Miss April." He flashed her a smile. "Might I have a word with you?"

"Why, yes!"

Polly wandered off a few feet. She didn't know what to think.

"Polly, cain you come help me? I'm needin' someone to spell me with Elvera whilst I git me a dollop more of the tater salad."

"Sure, Aunt Eunice." Polly took possession of the baby and sat in the grass. A few minutes later, April came up. She brought an overflowing plate and put it on the blanket. "I brought enough to share with you, Polly."

Her bright eyes and flushed cheeks made Polly take note. "What did the doctor have to say?"

"He's so nice, Polly."

"Yes, he is." Polly didn't have much of an appetite. It seemed the courtship she wanted was going to happen—but for April instead of herself.

"Haven't you noticed how he loves children?"

"Yes."

"And he's gentle. You can see it in his eyes and hear it in his voice."

Polly nodded.

"And sincere—he speaks from the heart. And his heart is in the right place."

Unable to speak, Polly nodded. *But my heart is in the wrong place. If he really prefers April, and April obviously cares for him, I should be happy for them. I don't understand, Jesus, how I misread this. I don't understand how You could let someone come into my life and win my respect and affection—even my love, only to intend him for some other woman.*

It felt like an eternity, April chattering all about what a wonderful man Dr. Eric Walcott was. Others sitting on nearby blankets chimed in to attest to his good qualities. Unable to hide her distress much longer, Polly slipped Elvera onto the blanket. "Excuse me."

She rushed off to the outhouse. It was the only place she'd get any privacy. A couple of minutes alone, and she scolded herself into composure. For years, Mama had taught her to keep her feelings hidden. Those lessons now served a completely different purpose.

Polly slipped from the outhouse and wandered off past a line of trees. She hoped for a little time and space of her own. Ever since her cousins had all moved in, she missed her privacy and times of solitude. If ever she needed them, it was now. Leaning against the trunk of a tree, she closed her stinging eyes.

Changes are always for the better if given to God. Daddy's wisdom filtered through her mind.

Lord, I have to give this to You.

"Polly?"

It was the doctor. She stiffened and didn't open her eyes.

"Aw, honey, not another headache," he said in a whisper-quiet voice. He moved close. His fingertips skimmed across her forehead.

How easy it would be to lie! It would let her save face. Someone would take her home and leave her alone in the dark where she could weep in utter privacy.

"Here. Sit down."

Her watery knees just gave way. Against her will, she opened her eyes. Doc knelt beside her, concern creasing his forehead. An armful of wildflowers lay strewn across her hem and at their feet.

He was gathering those for April. Her breath caught on that painful realization. Straining to maintain the slender thread of her composure, she whispered, "I really don't have a headache. I just wanted to be alone."

He sat back on his heels as a slow, low chuckle rumbled out of him. "With both clans together? You must believe in miracles."

She managed a wan smile.

"I hold a lot of faith, and I believe in miracles, Polly." He leaned to the side and scooped up several flowers. "Healing and loving are acts of faith."

She stared at the mariposa lilies, mustard, poppies, and shooting star in his strong, large hand.

"I once told you a handful of flowers didn't make a healer. You've taught me it's not the flowers—it's the hands God puts them in and blesses that makes the difference."

"Thank you."

He placed the flowers in her lap—all but one bunch of white buckwheat blossoms. "But today, I'm hoping for a different kind of miracle. I love you, Polly Chance."

Her heart leapt.

"Will you marry me?"

He'd just asked what she most wanted—and she'd given it to God. Polly looked at him in stunned silence.

His eyes sparkled. "I have your parents' blessing—I let you go saddle Blossom today just so I could be alone with them. If that's not enough, April's promised to bake us a spectacular wedding cake. I figured if I was going to be part of the family, I'd better get them on my side from the very beginning."

"My family loves you. . . ." She slid her hand up to his and took the flower. It looked like a simple, sweet bridal bouquet. "But not as much as I do."

"Well?" a voice prodded from not far away.

They both turned. Everyone stood around them. Polly and he had been so intent upon one another, they hadn't heard a thing.

"Polly's consented to be my wife."

"Well, then, what're ya waitin' on?" Uncle Obie asked. "Kiss the gal!"

Eric cupped her face and smiled. "Don't mind if I do."

Polly didn't mind, either.

epilogue

"You're going to be late," Aunt Delilah called through the door.

"It can't be helped," Polly called back as her gaze met Eric's.

"They can't do it without us," he said in a practical tone.

"I cain't do it without you, neither," Aunt Lois moaned. "I'm powerful sorrowed by that. Truly, I am."

"We aren't. We're glad to be with you." Polly wiped her aunt's face.

"Awww, merrrcyyy!" Lois curled up, grabbed Polly's hand, and bore down.

"Lord, help my Lois in her travail!" Uncle Obie groaned from beneath the window outside.

After that contraction, Eric went to the window and called out, "You keep praying, Obie. I'm glad you found the ax. Lois is grateful to have it under your bed today."

"And we're more'n grateful to the both of you fer bein' here with us today," Obie hollered back.

Polly smiled at her fiancé. He winked back. He'd learned to understand the oddities, rituals, and special ways of doing things for the people of Reliable, and now he didn't balk at mixing them with "sound medicine." He'd come a long way, and she loved him all the more for it.

"Merrrcyyy!"

"Oh, no!" Obie moaned from outside. He waited until his wife's contraction ended; then he cleared his throat. "Lois, we've got ourselves a problem. There was twelve disciples, but

I don't want no child of mine named Judas Iscariot."

Lois's beet-red face blanched. "This babe is our twelfth," she whispered to Eric.

"That's not a problem whatsoever," he soothed. "Acts chapter one speaks of the apostles deciding on a replacement for Judas. The choice was between Barsabbas, who was also called Justus, and Matthias. They cast lots, so Matthias won."

"Matthias'll do if hit's a man-child. What'll I do iff'n hit's a girl?"

"Matilda," Polly suggested.

"Merrrcyyy!" Lois bore down, then caught her breath. As Polly mopped her brow, Lois caught her hand. "Don't you dare go a-tellin' Obie 'bout those other two names. He'll want me to have two more children, and I'm plumb wore out."

"It'll be our secret," Polly said.

"Patients deserve privacy, after all." Eric's voice stayed low, but he wore a conspiratorial grin.

By the time they'd delivered baby Matilda and made sure mother and child were both stable, it was obvious Polly and Eric would arrive at the church thirty minutes late. He strode up to the altar, leaving Kate and April to keep guard in front of the door to the coatroom. Five aunts and Laurel all bumped around, dressing the bride.

"I just can't imagine this," Laurel fretted. "Bad enough, you're late to your own wedding, but don't you know it's bad luck for the groom to see the bride on their wedding day?"

"We don't need luck. We have love, and we have God." Polly felt her bun slipping.

"That you do," Mama said as she calmly reached up and tamed Polly's hair into submission and pinned the veil in place.

Her aunts and Mama all took their seats. Dressed in new lavender dresses, Kate and April walked down the aisle. Just before Laurel took her walk, she kissed Polly. "I'll mind them. Don't worry. And by the way—throw the bouquet to me!"

Step-by-step, holding Daddy's arm, Polly walked to the handsome doctor, to the love God had given her, and into her future.

A Letter To Our Readers

Dear Reader:
In order that we might better contribute to your reading enjoyment, we would appreciate your taking a few minutes to respond to the following questions. We welcome your comments and read each form and letter we receive. When completed, please return to the following:

Fiction Editor
Heartsong Presents
PO Box 719
Uhrichsville, Ohio 44683

1. Did you enjoy reading *Handful of Flowers* by Cathy Marie Hake?
   ❑ Very much! I would like to see more books by this author!
   ❑ Moderately. I would have enjoyed it more if

   _____

   _____

   _____

2. Are you a member of **Heartsong Presents**? ❑ Yes ❑ No
   If no, where did you purchase this book? _____

   _____

3. How would you rate, on a scale from 1 (poor) to 5 (superior), the cover design? _____

4. On a scale from 1 (poor) to 10 (superior), please rate the following elements.

   ____ Heroine   ____ Plot
   ____ Hero   ____ Inspirational theme
   ____ Setting   ____ Secondary characters

5. These characters were special because? _____

_____

_____

6. How has this book inspired your life? _____

_____

_____

7. What settings would you like to see covered in future
   Heartsong Presents books? _____

_____

_____

8. What are some inspirational themes you would like to see
   treated in future books? _____

_____

_____

9. Would you be interested in reading other **Heartsong
   Presents** titles? ❏ Yes ❏ No

10. Please check your age range:
   ❏ Under 18   ❏ 18-24
   ❏ 25-34   ❏ 35-45
   ❏ 46-55   ❏ Over 55

Name _____

Occupation _____

Address _____

City, State, Zip_____

MASQUERADE

4 stories in 1

*B*ehind one feathered mask, four women of three different eras are surrounded by treachery and deception, intricate ploys, ill-bred engagements, aristocractic crooks, fraudulent families, and a few poor choices of their own. But love also hides in well-disguised companions, and God has a purpose even when things seem impossibly complicated.

Historical, paperback, 352 pages, 5³⁄₁₆" x 8"

Heart♥ng

Presents